D1235284

SPECIAL MESSAGE TO READERS

This book is published under the auspices of

THE ULVERSCROFT FOUNDATION

(registered charity No. 264873 UK)

Established in 1972 to provide funds for research, diagnosis and treatment of eye diseases. Examples of contributions made are: —

A Children's Assessment Unit at Moorfield's Hospital, London.

•

Twin operating theatres at the Western Ophthalmic Hospital, London.

•

A Chair of Ophthalmology at the Royal Australian College of Ophthalmologists.

•

The Ulverscroft Children's Eye Unit at the Great Ormond Street Hospital For Sick Children, London.

You can help further the work of the Foundation by making a donation or leaving a legacy. Every contribution, no matter how small, is received with gratitude. Please write for details to:

THE ULVERSCROFT FOUNDATION,
The Green, Bradgate Road, Anstey,
Leicester LE7 7FU, England.
Telephone: (0116) 236 4325

In Australia write to:
THE ULVERSCROFT FOUNDATION,
c/o The Royal Australian and New Zealand
College of Ophthalmologists,
94-98 Chalmers Street, Surry Hills,
N.S.W. 2010, Australia

FREE FALL

Jennifer Gray, working with Colin Thomas on a sports promotion, doesn't like her job. He's a pilot, skydiver and owner of Skyway Aviation — and she's afraid of heights! Despite feelings of jealousy over Colin's love interest, he's not the man for her. However, Colin, knows a good thing when he sees it. So will his humour, sensitivity and old-fashioned charm help Jennifer overcome her fear of heights and convince her their relationship is just what she needs?

Books by Phyllis Humphrey
in the Linford Romance Library:

FALSE PRETENCES
TROPICAL NIGHTS

PHYLLIS HUMPHREY

FREE FALL

Complete and Unabridged

LINFORD
Leicester

First published in Great Britain in 2009

First Linford Edition
published 2011

British Library CIP Data

Humphrey, Phyllis A.
Free fall. - -
(Linford romance library)
1. Sports promoters- -Fiction. 2. Love stories.
3. Large type books.
I. Title II. Series
813.6–dc22

ISBN 978–1–4448–0920–6

Published by
F. A. Thorpe (Publishing)
Anstey, Leicestershire

Set by Words & Graphics Ltd.
Anstey, Leicestershire
Printed and bound in Great Britain by
T. J. International Ltd., Padstow, Cornwall

This book is printed on acid-free paper

1

It seemed like only yesterday that Jennifer's boss repeated, 'You're going to drive an *airplane* down the highway and park it in the *middle* of the mall?' As a matter of fact, it *had* been only yesterday.

Jennifer Gray stood on the tarmac of the small airport nestled in the sheltered bowl of California's San Joaquin Valley and fumed. She had less than an hour to get the plane she wanted into its slot at the Lido Lane Shopping Center for her sports promotion, and fog — with its chilling blasts of air — swirled like wet smoke across the pavement.

She hated airports. And, worse, airplanes. The Wright Brothers, as far as she was concerned, should have stayed on the ground and done something useful, like opening a fast food chain, something people *needed* back then.

Her knees met through the heavy fabric of her jeans, her toes curled in her short leather boots, and her hands burrowed deep in the pockets of her Irish knit sweater, the collar pulled up to just below the cold tip of her nose.

The fog, unusually heavy for June, had already obliterated everything — the hangars and planes had disappeared. It looked like a set from that old movie *Casablanca* and it didn't take much to imagine Humphrey Bogart and Ingrid Bergman stepping out of the fog, the darkness, and each others' lives.

A sound, reminiscent of the one made by her former vehicle, a finicky VW bug, shattered the air. Definitely a motor of some sort. She listened intently while it sputtered, then died completely, only to cough into life again. That was the thing about motors: they had a nasty habit of conking out. And although she had promised herself before — any number of times — she renewed her vow never to be lured into anything that used its motor to leave the ground.

The noise of the engine increased, and the nose of a small plane poked through the mist. That was the reason she had flunked Fear of Flying School. For a moment the pilot seemed intent on taxiing right up onto her toes, but then it stopped moving and the engine died.

The permit, folded deep in her purse, stated 'Cessna 150' and why she had ever expected it to be no larger than a sports car, she couldn't imagine. She had asked the gentleman on the phone for a *very* small airplane, and he had promised her one that carried only two people. So why then did this machine appear to be the size of a locomotive?

'Ken?' She peered into the darkness and mist but couldn't see anyone. Ken McGrath, maintenance manager of the shopping center, where the plane had to fit on the mall, had driven her there in his car and apparently wandered off somewhere. Maybe into one of the hangars to keep warm.

'No, the name's Colin Thomas.' The voice had a beautifully deep timbre to it. Darkness not withstanding, she then saw the man who belonged to it. Although his tanned face seemed at least ten inches above her own, she saw closely-cropped black curly hair, straight white teeth, broad shoulders and trim hips neatly wrapped up in a blue jumpsuit. Also, finely chiseled features, giving him an aristocratic appearance, which seemed somehow out of place on someone she assumed to be an airport mechanic. He was *definitely* not Ken McGrath. Or even Humphrey Bogart. But whoever this Colin Thomas was, he had no right to make her feel suddenly warm all over, in spite of the frigid air.

'Well, hello . . . ' he drawled. Before she could answer, he thrust his hand forward and caught hers, squeezing it firmly in a large, warm grip. His eyes, startlingly blue under thick dark lashes, widened.

Both his touch and his look made electric currents sizzle somewhere inside her. Seconds seemed to turn into hours. As much as she enjoyed the sensation, to say nothing of the approving looks the man gave her, she pulled her hand from his and kept her gaze on the abstract patch over the left breast pocket of his jumpsuit instead of his face.

He wasn't Ken — he was probably a mechanic who worked at the field — but perhaps he could shed some light on Ken's whereabouts.

'Have you seen a tall man,' she asked, 'fifty-ish, wearing a brown parka? His name's Ken McGrath.'

'Was he driving a green minivan?' He looked off in the direction of what could have been the parking lot.

'Yes.' Maybe he was waiting for her in the car.

'He's gone.'

'What?' She looked about, as if it were possible to see more than ten feet in front of her. 'He can't be gone. He has to drive me back to the Lido Lane

Shopping Center.'

'Brown coat? Green van?' The deep even tone had become unnervingly calm. 'Guy took off five minutes ago.'

'Oooh.' Jennifer gritted her teeth. 'What about a man named Whitey Franklin?'

She could tell by the man's expression that the news was all bad and she didn't need his, 'Gone, too, they drove off together,' to start an initial stage of panic. And why did Colin Thomas have to flash that drop-dead smile every time he said something she didn't want to hear?

'If you need a lift, I'll be glad to give you one.'

'You will?' His offer might possibly save her job and she considered dashing up and hugging him, but he began retreating toward the hazy outline of the Cessna. She followed, quickly, not to let him out of her sight. Two men had already disappeared on her.

When she reached the plane, he was standing beside one of the little doors and opened it for her.

'Hop in,' he said. Then he skirted the nose, went around to the other side, and slid into the pilot's seat.

Oh, no, he was not getting her into anything with wings. And he wasn't just a mechanic. He was obviously a pilot as well. 'That's a plane.'

'You noticed.' He leaned across the seat. 'I'm going to the center, and there's room for two.'

'Excuse me, but I can't do that. I — ' How could she tell this man about her phobia? She hated to admit it even to herself.

'I . . . um . . . have this thing about heights.'

'Heights?'

Jennifer nodded. 'You see, I'm afraid of them. It. Whatever.' Oops. Usually she never admitted her phobia, but somehow this man made her tongue loosen as if it had a mind of its own.

His laugh came out deep and throaty. 'The plane isn't going to leave the ground!' He sobered immediately. 'Don't be embarrassed. You have lots of company. Still, I find it hard to reconcile that with your arranging for our Cessna.'

'If it weren't for this mall promotion, I'd have nothing to do with an airplane, but . . . '

He reached across the empty seat and, before she could utter another sound, captured her elbow in one of his large, strong hands and coaxed her part way inside.

She was about to tell him she would rather call a cab, when she caught sight of her watch face. She should have been at the shopping center fifteen minutes ago. Now, *now* she had reason to panic.

'Come on,' he said, 'it will be something to tell your grandchildren about some day.'

She could hear him laughing softly as he leaned away from the empty seat, and — not because of his jibe, but because it had taken her two years after college to even break into public relations and two more to land the spot with Piedmont Productions — she made herself ease her hips through the open doorway and sit beside him. Seemingly of their own volition, her hands found the edge of the seat and closed tightly, like a hungry Venus Flytrap, around the smooth leather. As much as she had enjoyed looking at that handsome face before, she gazed straight ahead, toward at least a hundred menacing little dials and knobs on the dashboard. Or whatever they called that in an airplane.

His arm crossed in front of her and he pulled the door beside her closed. 'If you're still afraid, you can fasten your seat belt, even though the police escort won't allow us to drive over five miles an hour.'

The words penetrated her fear. Of course. She herself had arranged for two motorcycles in front and two behind to see that no one accidentally crashed into the plane while it made its trip up a highway instead of a runway.

All the same, she reached eagerly for the belt and pulled it into position across her hips. Surprisingly, the simple act calmed her fears somewhat. Really, she told herself, it was going to be just like riding in a car.

Then her pilot did something incomprehensible to the controls and the engine leapt into life again. Right away, the notion of riding in a car flew out the window and she felt a pulsing beat begin deep in the pit of her stomach, as if a little man in high-heeled boots were in there dancing a mad fandango.

'Mr. Thomas,' she said, suddenly feeling the need for more air, 'is there . . . ? I mean, it seems rather close in here.' She took several quick, shallow breaths.

Without taking his eyes from the instruments, he fished around behind the seat. 'Call me Colin, please,' he said, and handed her a used paper bag that, from the smell of it, had once held a tuna fish sandwich.

'What's this for?'

'If you're going to hyper-ventilate, breathing into a paper bag can help.'

The thought of breathing tuna fish

fumes made her want to laugh and she realized she was getting her lungs under control already. Then two motorcycle drivers pulled up alongside the plane and Colin maneuvered the craft into position behind them.

They were moving, and instead of feeling worse, she actually felt calmer. Was it because of her job — knowing she was responsible for bringing the plane to the mall — or was it Colin Thomas? He sat erect, the top of his head almost brushing the ceiling of the plane, his firm jaw tilted slightly upward. No doubt about it, strength and determination emanated from him. He was probably one of those unflappable types, spreading comfort and security around like a warm blanket. A tingling sensation began in her midriff. She dropped the bag back behind the seat.

She looked out the front window of the plane and saw the red lights of the two motorcycles blinking in the darkness. Colin moved the Cessna forward and they quickly left the confines of the airport and turned into the street that fronted Skyway Aviation. From there they would taxi up the frontage road and then cross the highway on an overpass, turn right and drive into the shopping center parking lot.

Nothing to it, she had once, in her naïveté, thought. Now she worried about all the things that could happen on this three-mile jaunt. What if some sleepy-eyed motorist saw this apparition and panicked, crashing into them? Oh, the folly of attempting something you knew nothing about.

'What did you say your name was?' Colin turned his head briefly in her direction. She liked his profile too.

'Jennifer Gray, of Piedmont Productions.'

'Pretty name. May I call you Jennifer?' Then, without waiting for an answer, he said, 'Are you in charge of the promotion at Lido Lane?'

She nodded. 'Yes.'

'Whose idea was it to put a plane on the mall?'

'Mine, believe it or not.' It had been her idea exclusively to feature a real airplane in the sports promotion for the shopping center. As if that were not enough to boggle anyone's mind, she had also insisted in a moment, not so much of weakness as *insanity*, upon being the one to supervise its progress to the mall.

'Since it's a four-day sports promotion,' she said, 'I thought a small plane would fit in with the exhibits. As you may have guessed, I don't fly in them myself, but I know other people like to. You, for instance.'

'Yep.' He gave a John Wayne drawl to the word.

The popular notion of pilots, at least from what Jennifer had heard, was that they were either arrogant and conceited or confirmed daredevils, and she wondered if this one would fit into either of those categories. But were they all this gorgeous?

'I suppose anything on the ground must seem too tame for you. Except maybe racing sports cars. Do you, by any chance, do that when you're not flying?'

'No, I jump out of airplanes. I'm a skydiver.'

Jennifer's stomach heaved at the very thought of it. If flying in airplanes was too frightening for her to attempt, then jumping out of them, even with a parachute, could take a Nobel Prize for folly.

'That's even worse,' she managed to say.

He didn't take offense. 'To someone with a fear of heights, I suppose it would seem that way.' His voice had none of the condescension she often encountered when people knew of her fear, and it surprised her. For a mechanic — or pilot or skydiver or whatever he was — he showed an unexpected compassion.

'Do you work for Whitey Franklin?' she asked then.

'No, in fact, he works for me. I own Skyway Aviation.'

Another surprise. The morning was certainly bringing its share of revelations.

'Usually,' he went on, 'I teach flying. Whitey runs the office for me most of the time and I just sign checks when he puts them under my nose.' He paused only a moment before continuing. 'But I'd rather talk about you. How did an attractive young woman who's afraid just to taxi in a plane get mixed up in a sports promotion?'

Jennifer shrugged. 'In public relations one *never* reasons why. Believe me, it could be a lot worse.'

'Like a contest to push peanuts up a hill with your nose?' He glanced sideways at her and Jennifer saw a glint of mischief in his blue eyes.

'It's been done. Along with roller skating from coast to coast, backwards.'

He laughed and the pleasant sound of it momentarily filled the tiny cockpit. She glanced out the window and noticed that the fog had evaporated and the sky had brightened above the distant hills.

As if he read her thoughts, he said, 'The fog's burning off already. It's going to be a sunny day.'

'I know the summer heat will soon settle into the valley and I love this part of California, but why are the mornings so cold?'

He grinned. 'I'll bet you're from Los Angeles.'

'I grew up there,' she said. 'But I don't miss the overcrowding of a big city, or the freeway drivers.'

She also made more money there in public relations, but didn't tell him that. She liked the open spaces of the valley, the farms and more identifiable seasons.

'Besides,' she said, 'if I ever feel the need, a four-hour drive will take me either to Los Angeles or San Francisco.'

He didn't reply and she discovered with surprise that the overpass was already in view. Skillfully Colin turned the plane onto the small bridge and applied extra power for the slight incline. Then they were down the other side and turned into the parking lot of the shopping center.

A flashbulb popped nearby. That would be the photographer she had hired, hoping to gain some free publicity for the event in the local newspapers.

Colin brought the Cessna to a stop and cut the engine. As Jennifer unfastened her seat belt, he climbed out of the plane, came around to her side and opened the door. Before she could slide the short distance to the ground, he put his hands on her waist and lifted her out.

'Here you are, safe and sound,' he said. 'You should congratulate yourself on what you just did. Okay, the plane didn't take off, but you were able to sit in it for almost thirty minutes without having a heart attack.'

He was not only right, but his touch and his fabulous smile made her heart do crazy loops and she couldn't speak.

A man approached and greeted Colin. Then he turned toward Jennifer.

'Hi, I'm Whitey Franklin.'

She hadn't met Whitey before but had spoken to him on the telephone when she made the arrangements for the airplane. She shook his outstretched hand.

'Jennifer Gray. I see where you get your nickname.'

The man grinned, running a hand through his thick white hair. He looked to be in his sixties, small and wiry.

'Have you spoken to Ken McGrath?' They were running behind schedule and Jennifer felt a moment's anxiety. 'He knows where I want the plane situated.'

Whitey nodded. 'We'll bring it onto the mall now.'

He left quickly and she turned to Colin. 'Thanks again for bringing the plane. If I ever get over my fear of flying, well — ' She reached out and briefly shook his hand, conscious of its delicious pressure against hers. ' — I'll look you up.'

Her words repeated themselves in her

head. She would never look him up, and, suddenly the thought of never seeing him again brought a stabbing pain to her chest. He was the first man in a long, long time who excited her. Why did he have to be so different? Why did opposites attract when no good could possibly come of it?

2

Jennifer turned to go, but Colin struck out across the lot with her. 'You'll look me up? Considering your present feeling about airplanes, that might be a long wait.' He matched his stride to hers. 'Anything I can do to help?'

'Thanks for the offer, but everything should be in place by now. If not, I'm in very serious trouble.'

'The truth is I don't know much about your line of work. So, if you don't mind, I'll just tag along.'

On one hand, she welcomed his company, but a tiny voice in the back of her mind whispered, 'Don't encourage him.' Ye gods, he lived in the sky!

'I'm afraid you'd find it very boring.'

'I promise not to say a word if you don't want me to, or you can string me up from a tree in my own parachute.'

She couldn't help smiling at him.

'Well, all right.' Just this once, what harm could it do if he strolled across the mall with her?

She walked through the opening between two large buildings where the sidewalk broadened into a wide outdoor mall, one story high, dotted with concrete planters containing leafy green trees, varieties of flowers, and an occasional modern metal sculpture. She had shopped there many times, since she lived in an apartment close by, but now she scanned it, not as a shopper, but as a promoter, visualizing where the various exhibits would be placed.

She checked the south end, noting that ramps were already in place so that vehicles could get over the curb, then headed in the opposite direction, almost a full city block, to where forest green tents sprouted on the concrete, along with booths that housed tennis and golf exhibits.

Colin stopped to admire a collection of dirt bikes and dune buggies. 'What do you think of these? No wings, no flaps, no propellers.'

'Too fast,' she answered.

'I'll bet golf is your game. You walk around for hours hitting a little ball into a hole in the ground. Didn't someone call it 'a good walk spoiled'?'

She shook her head. 'My father always said it's an old man's game, and I don't have the necessary qualifications.'

'Not by a long shot!' he said. 'Tennis then?'

'I play a little.'

'Ah, at last we have something in common.'

She didn't answer. Did she really want to find anything in common with him? Flying was quite bad enough, but he actually stepped out of planes and into the clouds.

Having reached the north end of the mall, she observed skis and snowmobiles making their appearance.

'You ought to like these,' he said. 'They never leave the ground. Well, not much.' Before she could reply, he parroted, 'Too fast.'

She just nodded, then turned around and headed back toward the east side from which they'd entered.

Colin continued to follow her. 'Tell me how a young lady — a very pretty young lady — who doesn't like anything that moves fast came to be handling a big sports promotion.'

Jennifer supposed her long hair blowing freely, and the fact that she wore pants instead of her usual tailored suit, made her seem younger than her twenty-six years. But his assumption didn't bother her. 'Just lucky, I guess.'

She felt no need to go into detail, even though his comment reflected her very own feelings on the subject. She had pleaded not to be given this assignment, but Peter Cramden, her new boss, brooked no arguments. He had been regional manager for only a month, and so eager to prove himself, that he had chosen Jennifer, of all people, to handle this promotion. Although she tactfully pointed out to him those with more qualifications, he countered by saying he thought any person in the company should be able to handle any assignment. There seemed to be an additional hint in his voice that if she didn't cooperate, he could find someone to take her place — permanently.

Colin went on. 'In addition, the newspaper said you'll have four sailboats, six power boats, two motor homes, and a complete log cabin on the mall today — '

'I know about the newspaper article,' Jennifer interrupted, impressed nevertheless that he could quote all the details. 'I wrote the story myself.'

'Did you?' Again he smiled appreciatively at her. 'That I can believe, but actually being in charge of running the whole thing doesn't seem to me a job for a young woman. A muscle-bound athlete maybe. You should be sitting in a garden listening to music and doing needlepoint.'

He could be astute, she'd give him

that. She'd said almost the same thing to her boss three weeks before. She hadn't obtained a liberal arts degree, studied literature, music, and drama for nothing.

'Okay, you're very perceptive. My previous assignments have been art showings, museum openings, and symphony performances.'

'Aha,' he gloated, 'I was right.'

'That one day I'd be asked to organize a sports promotion never entered my head.' She shrugged. 'But that's life in the promotion business.'

She changed the subject. 'Do you think they're having trouble with the plane?' She had expected the Cessna to come onto the mall by then, but remembered its earlier coughing fit or whatever it was.

He shook his head. 'It'll be here. If it fits.'

'What do you mean, 'if it fits'? It's not exactly a 747.' A queasy feeling started in her stomach.

She made a deliberate effort to calm

down, to slow the furious thumping of her heart. Sometimes, public relations seemed the most difficult job in the world. Being always polite, cajoling, compromising, could be very difficult, and almost always — in her experience — a man made it so.

'Maybe I'm wrong,' Colin said. 'Perhaps there's more room to maneuver than it seemed.'

Without waiting to hear more, she began to run — talk about too fast! — through the mall back to the parking lot, hardly noticing that Colin didn't follow her that time.

She found Whitey and McGrath, the middle-aged and usually jolly center maintenance manager, deep in discussion beside the plane, which hadn't moved a single inch.

'What's the matter?' she asked, thoroughly alarmed now.

'I was sure it would fit,' McGrath said.

'How?' Whitey asked. 'The fuselage will go through the opening, but not the wings.' He stalked to the back of the plane, squatted down and peered at the opening between the buildings, as if visualizing how it would fit between them.

'Maybe if you went sideways,' McGrath said. Then added sheepishly, 'But I guess you can't drive it in that way.'

Jennifer's spirits dropped into her boots. After all this trouble, would she have to leave the plane out of the exhibit? Colin Thomas had just hinted she might not get the plane on the mall. Could he be right? How had he known?

She joined the men in staring at the plane as if it would somehow reveal the answer to the problem. Then she spoke absently, thinking out loud. 'Too bad the wings don't fold up like they do for aircraft carriers.'

'That's not a bad idea,' Whitey said.

'But these wings don't fold.' The suggestion made Jennifer's voice rise. She might not know much about airplanes but she recognized a solid wing when she saw one.

'No, but we can take them off out here, push her onto the mall and then put the wings back on.'

'You can take the wings off? How long does it take to do that?' Her mood suddenly brightened.

'A couple of hours to take them off and a couple more to put them back on again.'

'But we don't have that much time.' Her tone rose an octave in spite of her efforts to remain calm. 'It's almost six o'clock now. Everything must be ready by nine thirty.'

'Maybe we can do it in a little less time.'

Holding her voice steady took effort. 'That's not all. This parking lot will be half full by nine. I can't have a major overhaul going on out here.'

'We can rope off this area of the lot,' McGrath said.

'That's not the worst of it. I need the plane in position before the other exhibits. If the boats and trailers arrive on the mall first, you'll never be able to maneuver the plane into place.'

'I'm sorry,' Whitey said, shaking his head. 'I guess we should have started out earlier this morning.'

Sure, and they could all have camped at the airport the night before. She fought down the temptation to blame someone: McGrath for assuring her the plane would fit between those buildings, herself for presuming he had measured the opening and given the dimensions to Whitey. Then they would have avoided this last minute disaster. It all came of not being familiar with this type of thing, she just couldn't anticipate everything. To say nothing of Murphy's Law that if anything *could* go wrong, it *would*!

But there was no point in getting upset. The men were doing their best to solve the problem.

'Okay,' she said, 'dismantle the wings. But please start now and do it as quickly as you can. When you have the plane inside, take it straight to its location in front of 'Soldier of Fortune,' before you put the wings back on. That should save some time.' She smiled encouragement at them. A successful public relations person was always cheerful, like a Boy Scout. But she hoped that her boss wouldn't come to the center to say, 'I told you so!'

Colin, who had reappeared midway in the discussion, came closer. 'Hold it,' he said to Whitey, who had already begun to pull out some tools. 'That isn't necessary.'

'I can't get the plane in any other way,' Whitey said.

'That's right.' Jennifer joined in. Having accepted Whitey Franklin's solution, she wanted to get on with it. She didn't need Colin Thomas — even if he was a Colin Firth look-a-like — to throw ice water on the plan. 'This is the widest opening onto the mall.'

'Maybe so, but I've just been around the center and there's another way.'

'There is?' Jennifer wondered if it was possible he had a knack for saving lives. Could he rescue her for the second time that day — before it was even six o'clock? First, though, perhaps she'd better listen to his solution.

'The area between the two buildings on the south side, where the planter sits, would be a better choice.'

Her sudden elation fizzled. 'The distance between the building and the sculpture that stands in that planter is much narrower than this opening. If it won't fit through here, it certainly won't fit through there.'

'It will if you raise the plane. There's a ramp on that side already, next to the curb. All you have to do is put the ramp against the planter ledge, push the tail gear of the plane onto that, and keep the front gear off the ground. The three of us can manage that. Then the wings will clear the sculpture.'

As he spoke, she visualized his proposal. It might just work. At least she had to let him try. She had to get that plane onto the mall. 'It sounds like a possible solution,' she said at last. 'Let's try it.'

Whitey and McGrath moved quickly to the back of the Cessna, leaving Jennifer alone with Colin. 'It hadn't occurred to me to consider raising the wings,' she said.

'Perfectly understandable,' Colin said, taking her fingers in his, and speaking quietly, intimately. 'You'd just been in a plane for the first time and can't be expected to know about these things. I'm glad I came along this morning. I think this may be the beginning of a beautiful friendship.' He squeezed her hand. His touch and his look made electric currents sizzle somewhere inside her. Okay, so he quoted a line from *Casablanca*. Somehow she knew that her idea of a beautiful friendship did not in the least coincide with his. And, for that matter, she was certain she didn't want any kind of relationship with him. No matter what he thought, she would have nothing to do with a man who liked everything she hated.

'You could at least thank me,' he said.

'Thank you.' Her words barely audible, she tried to slip her hand from his, but instead he pulled her tightly to him. The feel of his thighs against hers, the sight of his mouth only inches away, drove every sensible thought from her head. His kiss was sweet, yet like no other she had ever had before, leaving her breathless and wanting more.

He released her and she came back to earth, realizing her reaction to him spelled danger with a capital 'D.' If only they had got the plane on the mall as originally planned. If only Whitey had driven it over instead of this skydiver. If only she'd never laid eyes on him.

Well, she consoled herself, retreating toward her office, she'd never have to see him again. Sure, he had made her feel like Ingrid Bergman or Bridget Jones or some other movie heroine, but that was her choice and she intended to stick with it.

But her lips still throbbed from his kiss and her pounding heart was saying just the opposite.

3

Peter Cramden perched on one corner of Jennifer's wide walnut desk, turned his head and gave her a Cheshire-cat smile. She knew he expected her to share his pleasure, and she was trying her best to give that impression.

'I said everything would fall into place perfectly.' His gray eyes reflected not only his delight that the Lido Lane project had turned into a tremendous success, but also his confidence in her ability. 'It was a great promotion.'

Never had she worked so hard planning anything, putting in three incredible weeks of effort for the event at the shopping center that lasted only four days. And now, on Monday morning, her boss's compliments made her uneasy. Only she knew that one part of the exhibit hadn't 'fallen' as perfectly as Peter imagined — getting that darn airplane on the mall. If it hadn't been for Colin Thomas, the *pièce de résistance* of her promotion might have collapsed like a souffle on a cattle drive.

And she had been unable to stop thinking about Colin ever since. She remembered clearly every word they'd spoken to one another. If she had any interest in getting involved with a 'hunk,' she'd had her chance. Knowing her aversion to his type did nothing to stem the desire he'd awakened in her. With effort, she thrust the vision aside.

'You brought it off so flawlessly,' Peter continued, 'I knew you were right for that assignment.' He left her desk and paced the floor, hands gesturing for emphasis. 'And I have something you'll like even better.'

She wondered why he thought she liked the sports idea in the first place. If she'd been with the agency ten years instead of only two, he'd never have talked her into it.

'I want you to imagine this,' he

continued, facing her, his back to her office windows. 'Six weeks of promotion on one central theme. It's something that's never been done in this part of the state before.'

Jennifer, who had been feeling something akin to embarrassment over his effusive compliments, felt a sudden wave of excitement. 'Do you mean the opera promotion? I already have some ideas I'd like to discuss with you.'

'I like to play hunches,' he said, on a roll now, ignoring her comment. 'Most of the time they pay off. What you did out there at Lido Lane, for example, proved that you needed more variety.'

Variety. Why was it that, suddenly, she no longer liked the sound of that word? 'What is it you have in mind?' Something about his pronouncement raised more than a slight suspicion that she didn't really want to know.

'You'll love it,' he said.

'Love what?' She *knew* she was going to hate it.

'Skydiving.'

Skydiving? Another sports theme, and a ridiculous sport at that.

Peter, apparently oblivious to Jennifer's smile having turned to open-mouthed incredulity, went on. 'It will feature Colin Thomas. I've heard he's the best skydiver in the entire country, maybe the world. He placed second in international competition year before last.'

If the news of the skydiving exhibition had turned her body to ice and immobilized her lips, then that last remark could easily put her into a state of terminal coma. Colin Thomas, of all people, the first man in ages to make her feel desirable, and who she expected never to see again. Yet the vision floated before Jennifer's unwilling eyes: midnight-black curly hair, blue eyes, a smile that could undermine the determination of a hard-boiled police-woman. A man whose occupation sent chills of fear through her.

'Skydiving? How — how interesting,' she managed to say. The last thing you did at Piedmont Productions — just before handing in your resignation, that is — was protest too strongly about an assignment. Oh, in theory you lobbied — diligently — for events in your field of expertise or interest, but in actual fact Peter made decisions that were as close to inevitable as death and taxes.

'How did you ever happen to think of that?' She was making conversation, trying to collect her thoughts sufficiently to think of a way to squirm out of it.

'I've you to thank for it,' he said. 'I met Colin at your promotion last week and he gave me the idea.'

Colin gave him the idea? Jennifer felt light-headed, but Peter, oblivious to her distress, paced around the room, hands shoved into his trouser pockets, and no doubt congratulating himself on his latest coup.

It gave her an opportunity to exchange her forced smile for a look that would explode dynamite, which, fortunately, he couldn't see. Thank her?

She had accepted the sports promotion, did a good job, and look where it got her!

Drat that Colin Thomas, anyway. It wasn't bad enough that he was the most sensational man she had met since moving to the valley and had a life-style she wouldn't emulate for a fortune in diamonds, but his having saved her pride by getting that mechanical monster onto the mall still rankled. Now Peter expected her to work with him for at least six weeks.

'Peter,' she began, softly. 'I realize this is — '

'Oh, don't thank me,' he said, turning to her. 'You deserve it. You did such a fantastic job last weekend, you'll probably be nominated for a Stanley Award at the annual banquet. It's the least I could do.'

Once more Jennifer's smile froze on her face, even while her lungs were working like a bellows run amok. She deserved it, did she? Whatever happened to the art shows, concerts and museum openings that her background and education cried for? And, worst of all, whatever happened to the opera promotion?

'Peter, I appreciate your confidence in me, but I only did the sports promotion for you because I wanted to cooperate. I wasn't qualified then and I'm not now.'

Peter spoke kindly, but firmly. 'Come now, you're not going to tell me that you're incompetent when you managed to put on one of the best promotions I've ever seen? You just need to have your mind challenged.'

Unfortunately, it wasn't only her mind Colin challenged. With a great effort, she composed herself. She'd have to think of a better way to solve this dilemma.

'I'm certainly glad it turned out well,' she said, softening her voice, realizing that she could hardly tell Peter why she never wanted to see Colin Thomas again. 'But I already have another promotion I'm working on, remember?'

'The opera company? I haven't forgotten.' His voice, while not exactly flat, lacked enthusiasm. 'Have you arranged funding for it? At our last discussion you told me that both federal and state money had dried up.'

Dejected, she had to admit that nothing had changed *vis a vis* the money needed to launch a season of opera in the valley. 'But I'm working on soliciting private funds,' she added, mentally ticking off a list of CEOs within a fifty mile radius known to have a positive cash flow. A big one.

'That could take a long time,' Peter said. 'Meanwhile you can do the skydiving exhibition. Thomas was so impressed with your ability, he asked for you specifically.'

The butterflies that had invaded her stomach at the thought of seeing Colin Thomas again turned into giant bees. Arguments sprang to mind, if not to her lips, her seniority being only slightly higher than the office coffee machine. The public relations field, never an easy one to break into, had become even more overcrowded since the severe cutbacks in Silicon Valley, and at least a dozen women would probably put their rivals' lives in danger if it meant having her job. She had worked too hard those nineteen months carving a niche for herself to blow it now by being stubborn.

But she had one Ace up her pink silk sleeve — Peter liked her. Not romantically. He was happily married, but, still in his thirties, the youngest man in the organization to have reached the title of Manager, his goal was to encourage other young people with new concepts. And Jennifer's innovative ideas always intrigued him.

'You've seen my plans for the opera promotion,' she reminded him. When he didn't answer, she continued. 'Piedmont Productions — ' and you, as manager, she thought, hoping he'd catch the implication, ' — will gain a lot of prestige if we can bring an opera company here. Everything is ready to go. It only requires the money.'

'I'm aware of that, but in the meantime this job needs work, and, frankly, I think you can bring some new and exciting twists to it.'

She could start by twisting Peter's neck. The thought almost made her laugh and she looked out the window. She was dangerously close to mutiny, yet excuses continued to pile up in her head. Then she remembered her former job in Los Angeles, her tiny cubicle of work space and how everyone joked that you'd know when you arrived because you'd have an office with a window. Well, she had her office now, with *two* windows. And a secretary besides, who sat in another room and typed her correspondence, threw out her junk mail, and screened her telephone calls. So she was a big fish in a little pond — it was what she wanted. Why was she trying so hard to scuttle her own ship?

Colin Thomas was why. Something told her she'd rue the day she ever got mixed up with him.

She turned around again, smiled sweetly at Peter, and played her last card. 'I really appreciate your confidence, and I'll do my best, but I hope you'll understand that I consider myself committed to the opera promotion whenever I can get funding.'

'Of course,' he said, coming toward her and stretching out his hand, as if to seal the bargain. 'That goes without saying. I promise.'

'Thank you.' She moved around him to her desk, where she riffled some papers as if anxious to get back to work.

'That's settled then,' Peter concluded, heading for the door. 'By the way, they're expecting you out at Skyway Aviation any time after two o'clock.'

'This afternoon?' She sat down in the chair, her legs suddenly limp as cooked spaghetti.

'Yes, I promised you'd begin work on it right away.'

She threw up her hands in surrender.

'Why not?' She smiled through clenched teeth, watched him leave and checked her watch. At least she still had something left of the morning, and she intended to use those too few precious minutes making some telephone calls on behalf of the opera promotion. Somehow she'd find the necessary funding to make the project feasible. Then perhaps her personal stock in the company would rise and she wouldn't be forced to take any more dumb assignments like skydiving.

She had barely pulled out her list of wealthy art patrons when Peter's secretary came into the room. 'These are for you,' she said, dropped a hefty pile of papers on Jennifer's desk, and left. The top one told her unmistakably about the subject matter. It was a glossy photograph of Colin Thomas, wearing a parachute over his jumpsuit and a helmet tucked under one arm, a vast sweep of blue sky behind him. If she were anyone else, his smile would entice her to start a skydiving career the next day.

Her stomach contracted. How ironic.

With at least a million skydivers hanging around airports all over the world, it was her own promotion — her insistence on having an airplane on the mall — that enabled Peter to meet Colin and set this up. Was Peter an unwitting matchmaker, or was Fate forcing her into proximity with a man who made her feel all squishy inside? Notwithstanding the kiss she could not forget, she vowed that she would resist his charms and stick strictly to business. Definitely.

4

After a lunch of minestrone and salad at Stone Soup near her office, Jennifer got into her car and struck off in the direction of the airport. One of the best things about her job was that, notwithstanding the two windows, she spent so little time in the office. It allowed her the freedom to enjoy the trees cloaked in bright green leaves that arched overhead and the June flowers scenting the air. She liked the town of Stafford and so far had no regrets that her work had brought her there.

She had made the right decision to leave L.A., only occasionally returning to visit her widowed mother who somehow seemed oblivious to the smog and congestion. Perhaps because she was so wrapped up in her own career as a film editor and her charity work. Jennifer resembled her mother in that way. Ever since high school, she'd volunteered her time to read to the blind. In fact, making cassette tapes for blind students had brought her into public relations work, and eventually put her in charge of charity promotions, getting paid for something she enjoyed.

Well, enjoyed up to now, anyway. Colin Thomas seemed to have a knack for single-handedly destroying it.

Immersed in her thoughts, she almost missed the turnoff to the airport. At the last moment, she pulled off the highway toward the red and white 'Skyway Aviation' sign and parked near their redwood-sided building. The small office she entered contained a broad counter blocking half the space, but no occupants.

She waited a few minutes, rapped her knuckles lightly on the counter and waited again, but still no one appeared. She slithered around the counter and, noticing another door at the rear of the office, opened it. It led to the airfield, and she strolled toward the hangars.

Before her sat planes of various types and sizes, and just seeing them at close range made her nervous. Several men dressed in coveralls worked on some of the planes, or just stood about, talking. But no Colin Thomas.

Farther out, where the black stretch of tarmac ended, three young girls wearing tee-shirts and jeans ran across the field, accompanied by a man in a tan jumpsuit. From his pale hair shining in the sun, Jennifer recognized Whitey Franklin. They stopped near a circle drawn on the ground and peered up at the sky. Curious, Jennifer looked up too.

A small plane, very much like the one she had ridden in to the shopping center mall, flew above, and then something fell from an open door on its side, grew larger. It was a man, his arms and legs outstretched as if to embrace the ground when he hit it. Reason told her he had jumped out of the plane deliberately and would open his parachute, yet down and down he came, as if he'd never stop falling. Terror crept up her spine. She couldn't bear to look, yet her gaze refused to leave the man.

Perspiration popped out on her forehead and neck, threatened to soak the back of her dress. Her heart pounded, her hands felt clammy. When she thought she couldn't stand it another minute and wanted to scream, something attached to the jumper's back leaped upward and Jennifer saw a tiny white piece of cloth that resembled a miniature parachute. Even before she could wonder how he'd be saved from certain death by something as small as that, the small chute pulled more fabric out of the backpack, and then a beautiful orange and white striped canopy blossomed above the figure. As it billowed out in the sky, the man was jerked from his horizontal position into an upright one, and slowly glided toward earth.

Riveted to the scene above her, Jennifer's senses returned to near-normal, her body relaxed, her breathing resumed. The jumper slowly became larger and then she realized his canopy was not solidly round. Huge empty spaces gaped between the gores.

She ran to Whitey's side. 'That parachute has holes!'

Franklin turned his head and acknowledged her. 'Of course. That's how he guides it. Air comes in through the openings and when he pulls on the lines, it makes the parachute change direction. Actually, that's a very old type. No one uses them anymore. Watch now. In a moment he'll land right here. He never misses a target.'

Sure enough, the skydiver descended lower and lower and then landed right in the center of the circle, his knees flexing as he touched it. Immediately on landing, he pulled the collapsing parachute to the ground. The young girls ran over to him, but Jennifer stood still, calming down after the excitement of witnessing her first parachute jump. She had seen brief shots of skydiving in films, but it never moved her. In fact, she only thought it stupid — jumping out of a perfectly good airplane — but there was something awe-inspiring about seeing it live. The immediacy of the danger and her reaction to it had come as a total surprise. Instead, she continued to stare. He finished rolling the parachute into a manageable bundle, the girls walked off, giggling, and he came toward her, removing his helmet. With a mixture of fear, embarrassment, and, she grudgingly admitted, total admiration, she recognized Colin Thomas.

He stood in front of her, smiling down, while her heart — not fully recovered from her fear he would kill himself — felt as if infatuation had not only hit her hard, but dragged her a mile as well.

She took a deep breath. 'That was — wonderful.' Well, she had to say something complimentary to someone who'd just plunged to earth as casually as if he were taking a bus across town. Didn't she?

'Thank you.' Colin's smile at seeing Jennifer never varied, and he handed his rolled-up chute to Whitey, who walked off the field with it, leaving them alone.

'You surprise me,' he said. 'Peter told me the exhibition was going forward, but I was afraid you might persuade someone else to take it. You seemed rather less than pleased with me when we parted at Lido Lane last week.'

Jennifer walked back toward the office building beside him. 'Unfortunately, I don't have that kind of clout.'

'Unfortunately?' he repeated.

'That exhibit last weekend was my first venture into the world of sports. This is my second, not exactly a lot of expertise, wouldn't you say?'

'Your exhibit on the mall was fantastic. If you didn't know what you were doing, you could've fooled me. You'll be great on this tour.'

She laughed. 'I, the lady who's afraid of heights?'

'That's right. I forgot about that.' He

stopped walking and frowned slightly, as if an idea suddenly occurred to him. Then, without another word, he took her hand and led her toward the runway.

'What are you doing? Where are we going?' She had to run to keep up with his long strides.

'I'm going to help you overcome that,' he said over his shoulder. 'Trust me, this will work.'

'What will work?' She tried to stop, but his momentum didn't allow it and instead she merely stumbled in her high heels. His hand went under her elbow, holding her up, and he continued his giant steps. Even while trying to keep from tripping again, she realized he was leading her to the airplane which had just landed, no doubt the same one from which he'd just made his jump.

Suddenly the meaning of his words became clear and she felt as if her life were draining from her body. He planned to take her up and force her to parachute from the plane to overcome her fear of heights. Breath caught in her throat. 'You wouldn't!' she gasped.

'Why not?'

'I've never done it before. I couldn't possibly!'

'I know that,' he said, 'but there's a first time for everything.'

'I can't jump from a plane!' she shouted at his back.

He stopped dead in his tracks, the suddenness almost knocking her down, and turned a shocked gaze on her.

'Jump? Do you actually think I'd let you jump? That's the craziest thing I've ever heard.'

'But, I thought — I mean — ' Jennifer felt thoroughly confused, even as relief flooded over her.

Colin studied her face and then relaxed and smiled. 'Either you know even less about skydiving than I thought, or else you have an excessively low opinion of me.'

She merely stared at him, feeling embarrassed.

His look of outrage changed suddenly and he grinned. 'Do I look like the beast from forty fathoms?'

She remained silent and made a futile attempt to smooth her hair. She had worn it pinned back that day but it had come loose on her walk — make that run — across the field with Colin.

'Well, I can't blame you,' he said. 'I should have explained. But I wouldn't let my worst enemy make a jump without training, certainly not a beautiful woman like you.'

Jennifer tried not to let his compliment get to her. Not that she was having much success, but she had determined not to be affected by his good looks and charisma.

'Then what did you mean?' She gave up the attempt to put her hair back in order and pocketed the clips.

'I merely planned to take you for a short ride.'

'I can't do that. You wouldn't ask me if you realized I might throw up all over the upholstery.'

'It wouldn't be the first time,' Colin joked. 'Look,' he persisted, 'you'll have to overcome this fear gradually. You've already been in a plane on the city streets. The next step is to go up for a short ride.'

'You don't understand. People have tried to cure me of this before. I even took one of those 'Fear of Flying' courses a couple of years ago.'

'Well then — '

'I flunked.'

Colin looked at her a long while. Then his voice was soft, his tone sensible. 'It's not normal not to fly nowadays. You put yourself at a terrible disadvantage.'

'Don't you think I know?' Jennifer had seldom talked about her fear to others, and she didn't know why she felt she could confide in this particular man, except maybe that if she didn't explain he might take her up against her will. 'I'd love to be able to fly in airplanes. I've always dreamed of traveling to exotic places.'

'There are cruise ships.'

He was finding excuses for her. 'And there are cars and trains all over the world, too. I know that. But it's not the easiest or fastest way. You may not believe this, but I actually like to do adventurous things.'

'As long as you don't go too high or too fast.'

'Exactly. But I'd like to. Furthermore, the most important reason is that my job might require me to go somewhere in a hurry some day. I can't see myself turning down an assignment because I won't get in an airplane.'

'Well, then, let's get started. Do what's comfortable. You actually sat in the plane last week and it moved. That wasn't so terrifying, was it?'

'Well, I survived.'

'At the end I could have sworn you enjoyed yourself.'

She gave him a look of scorn and he continued hastily, 'Okay, you didn't. But if you're serious about overcoming this problem, you're going to have to push yourself a little. Get in the plane and taxi with me.'

'I've already done that.'

'How safe could you be? We were on a city street and you knew the plane wouldn't take off. This time you should taxi to the runway. We won't go up, but it will put you one step closer to the day you can do that. What do you say?'

Something about Colin gave her more assurance than she'd imagined possible. Not even in that class of twenty-five other people with the same problem had she felt as confident as she did right then. 'All right.'

'Great!' He took her hand again and led her toward a group of planes on the field.

'Do you have anything with eight engines?' she asked.

Grinning, he took her to a twin-engine plane with the name Beechcraft on the side. 'This is the best I can do right now, but since we're not taking off, what difference does it make?' His hand went under her elbow to assist her.

She was acutely aware of having to take a rather large step up into the plane, made awkward since she wore a dress that day. She wanted to clutch her skirt to her thighs, but instead had to hold onto a support.

'Yes, indeed,' Colin drawled, 'I think I'll drive this baby very slowly. Can't risk damaging legs like those.'

Jennifer smiled at the compliment, but thankfully the skydiver couldn't see her face. He closed the door and went around to the other side, climbing in beside her.

He fastened his own seat belt and then made sure she had fastened hers, but the old fear began to creep up on her. She had to get hold of herself, look at the instruments. But they only panicked her — she simply couldn't concentrate. He turned switches and dials, the engine caught, making a horrendous noise that almost drowned out her thoughts, and the Beechcraft moved forward.

She had lived through this part before, and even though her temperature seemed to be rising, she reminded herself that it wouldn't be much different from that other time. She forced herself to look out the window in front of her and watch the asphalt road edged with dry brown grass slip away under them. They taxied for a long time, it seemed, Colin true to his word to go slowly. Then the plane turned and stopped, and she stared down the length of a long black ribbon of runway, ending in distant green trees and a cobalt-blue sky unbroken by any clouds.

'Step number two completed,' Colin said in a voice like a Houston command controller. 'Step three coming up.'

'What's step number three?' She hoped her temperature would remain normal no matter what he said.

'I take off and circle the field once and land again. Five minutes tops. What do you say?'

Jennifer mentally checked her body.

Her breathing was almost normal. Her heart rate had calmed down to only a thousand or so beats per second. Maybe she could do it.

'I'll try,' she heard herself say. Was that her talking or was she just trying to impress this guy?

'Good girl.' His smile could have made the Statue of Liberty respond, and then he turned his attention back to the controls, picking up a microphone that hung from the dashboard and saying something to the control tower. Then the engines shrieked and the plane tore down the runway.

Jennifer's head moved backwards, thrown by the sudden acceleration of the plane, but her hand went out and clutched Colin's arm. 'I can't. Stop. Please stop!'

The application of brakes threw her head forward, blood rushed into a face that moments before had been cold with fear. Colin slowed and took the first exit off the runway, then spoke again into the microphone, even though he had to take her hand — in its deathlike grip — with him.

After they taxied briefly, he turned off the engine. In the silence, he said, 'Well, scratch step number three.'

'I'm sorry,' she said in an all-but-inaudible whisper, and noticed her legs had begun to tremble. Fear or relief?

He reached across her with his free hand, unfastened her seat belt and reached for the door handle. 'You'll have to let go of me now, so I can get out.'

Gently, he pried her fingers loose, placing her hand on a support, climbed from the cockpit and came around to her side. He put his hands on her waist and lifted her from the plane, setting her feet on the tarmac in front of him. Instantly, her arms went around his neck and stayed there.

For several moments neither of them moved, but finally she spoke. 'I feel like such a jerk.'

'You can't prove it by me. When a pretty girl puts her arms around me, I only think of her good taste — or my good fortune.'

'I'd let go, but I'm afraid I'll fall. My legs are so wobbly I could get a job in a circus as a rubber man.'

'Rubber woman,' he corrected, letting his hands slide more tightly across her back, making it sizzle with heat. 'If *I* were a jerk,' he continued, 'I'd take advantage of this. I might convince myself you're about to faint and give you mouth-to-mouth resuscitation.'

She didn't speak and his lips came close to hers.

'But I'll just be honest and say I want to kiss you.'

'I appreciate your honesty, and I'll be honest, too. I really don't think that's a good idea.' Her tone as cold as her flushed face and wildly beating heart permitted, still she couldn't move. She could only think of that other kiss and how much she wanted the thrill of it again.

Then he bent his head to hers and this time the kiss was not soft and sweet as the other had been, but firm and passionate, bringing her to a fevered wildness unmatched by anything in her past. Time stood still.

Finally reason kicked in. Why was she letting this man kiss her? She released her hold and pushed herself away from him. Her legs became almost normal once more, and she staggered back to the office of Skyway Aviation, not knowing if Colin followed her. She had one thought now. How would she ever manage to work with him for six weeks?

5

Back inside the building, the picture of an angel painted on a door caught Jennifer's eye, and hoping to find the ladies' room, she went in. Breathing rapidly, she noticed her heart seemed to be tap-dancing as if it were in a Busby Berkeley movie. Colin's kiss had caused an intense reaction, sweaty palms being the least of it.

She stared at herself in the mirror. Her sun-streaked tousled hair framed her flushed face, and she set about putting the long silky strands back into a twist, digging out the clips from her dress pocket. Keeping her hands busy gave her time to calm down and figure out what to do under these changed circumstances. Obviously they were attracted to one another.

It was bad enough that he looked on her as a young, stupid girl, incompetent to handle her job. And she'd soon prove him wrong on that score! But to kiss her just because he wanted to was insulting, as if he had no regard for her feelings in the matter.

The worst part of it had been her reaction to his kiss. Her traitorous body had responded to his sheer animal magnetism against her will. Yet, if he actually felt drawn to her, he had certainly chosen a poor way of showing it. But then, that kind of man probably knew nothing about gentleness. Colin seemed more eager to offend than to please. He had probably decided to alienate her, either with unpleasant behavior or unwanted attentions, so that she'd resign from handling his skydiving promotion. She already knew the man could change his behavior from Hyde to Jekyll at the blink of his black eyelashes.

Pushing the memory of being in his arms — something that would never happen again — into a far corner of her mind, she forced her professionalism to take over. She had to work with the man and she would. After all, she was no simpering schoolgirl. She could certainly keep Colin in his place, and that place was in the sky, not in her arms.

She didn't like the situation any more than he did, and if she could learn to live with it, so could he. In a few moments, she felt ready to tackle the ogre again, took a deep breath and left the room.

* * *

Colin sat at a desk behind the counter, waiting for Jennifer to return, wondering what his next move should be. He'd certainly bungled this affair so far. The trouble was she didn't react to him like other women. Okay, so she had responded to his kiss — she hadn't slugged him — but otherwise she seemed definitely turned off by him personally *and* by what he did for a living. He had to admit that made the challenge even more exciting. He'd have to change tactics, though.

He tilted his chair back and absent-mindedly ran fingers through his hair. A strong part of him didn't want to subdue this woman, turn her into another adoring fan. Was he growing up at last, finally tired of the game? But there had never seemed to be another choice. He was never going to marry, never have a child whose life he'd make miserable as his had been, and all those airport groupies made casual sex so easy.

But even if he considered Jennifer Gray off limits, he still had to work with her. So which would it be, another frontal assault or . . . ?

He got to his feet when he saw her coming. 'Miss Gray, please let me apologize. I know I was out of line back there.'

She paused a moment, then said crisply, 'Apology accepted. Let's forget it now and get down to business.'

But he didn't seem able to let it drop.

'I've certainly bungled our relationship so far. The trouble is I'm afraid what I do for a living — although it obviously turns you off — makes most women my adoring fans.'

'Like rock band groupies, you mean?'

'Exactly. Great for the ego, but, I'm beginning to think, perhaps a little juvenile. Can it be I'm growing up at last?' He struck his forehead playfully and laughed.

'You're free to do whatever you choose. Don't change your life-style on my account. So long as you don't involve me,' she added.

He neither affirmed nor denied her accusation. 'You make it very difficult for me to acquire the proper repentant attitude.'

'You don't have to repent for my sake. Just acknowledge that I know my job and let me do it without any more problems.'

'Kissing you isn't a problem. I'd call it spectacular. But, yes, I'm resigned to your handling the tour.'

'Peter said you asked for me and I agreed,' she said.

'So you did.' He smiled. 'In that case, I'll assume you enjoyed my kiss!'

'I didn't mean that!' she said quickly, her face reddening. 'I meant . . . '

'I know what you meant,' he interrupted. 'I'm willing to work with you as the public relations person on my tours, but I can't absolutely guarantee that I won't forget occasionally and try to kiss you again.'

'Do you consider it some sort of challenge?'

'Perhaps. I've never believed in taking life too seriously. One has to live each moment to the fullest, and I don't like to think of missing out on too many pleasant experiences.'

'I doubt you ever miss any,' she said.

He laughed again. 'Tell me how you became such a serious person so young. Were you raised in poverty and had to fight your way to the top?'

'No, I come from an ordinary middle-class family. Besides working for

Piedmont Productions, I do volunteer work. I think character and integrity are important traits.'

'Admirable, I'm sure,' he said, 'but I'm afraid you're getting too serious again. Somehow I don't want to talk about character and integrity when I'm with you.' His glance took in her entire form and he grinned. Then, in spite of his earlier words, he became serious.

'However, you're kinder to me than I deserve. I won't bore you with the details of how I became such an insensitive jerk, but I certainly shouldn't have taken my frustrations out on you. I'm sorry.' He paused, waiting for her answer.

Perhaps realizing his apology had not come easily, and ready for a truce, she said, 'You're forgiven.'

'Look here, since we're going to work together, may I call you Jennifer?'

Since he had already kissed her, she laughed at the irony. 'I probably can't stop you.'

'And I promise not to make any more chauvinistic comments. I'm sure you're very good at your job.'

He pointed to the worn leather swivel chair and sat down opposite her.

'At least you're not resigning from the tour, and I really meant that apology.' He paused, then added, 'But I won't promise not to at least *want* to kiss you again. If you need any more resuscitation, that is.'

Her grin helped. 'My only need at the moment is to understand skydiving enough to handle this tour properly.'

'I'm glad Peter gave this assignment to you.'

'After I told you how inept I felt at handling that Lido Lane event, I find it hard to imagine why you do.'

'But today lots of women love sports, even the sports normally considered male-dominated.'

'I know they do. I just don't happen to be one of them. Maybe because I was an only child and my father didn't think girls needed sports in their lives. I didn't even have a bicycle until I was ten.'

'That's too bad. But girls are in Little League now and women are becoming skydivers. I've trained seven myself.' He paused. 'Surely you heard about the 151 women who broke a skydiving record with a formation over Perris Valley.'

'Yes, I believe I read that, and I'm glad to hear it, but you're still not going to make a convert out of me.'

His gaze traveled over her face. 'Actually, aside from your fear of heights, I thought I noticed a little defensiveness on your part, as if you weren't exactly overjoyed with the assignment for some other reason.'

She looked down a moment, fingering the folds in her skirt, as if forming an answer. Maybe she didn't want him to think she wouldn't be enthusiastic about his tour and do her absolute best.

'My background hasn't been in these areas, but promoting is promoting.' She shrugged. 'In that respect, a sports event is not much different from say, an opera benefit.'

As soon as she mentioned it, Colin made the connection. 'I knew there was something. You'd rather be doing an opera benefit than this?'

When she didn't answer immediately, he added, 'Is there such a promotion and did you get switched out of it and into mine against your will?'

She looked up at him. 'It's not like that at all. The opera benefit might never begin. There are funding problems. But if it does, I've been promised I can supervise it. Now, let's get down to our own business — '

But he refused to budge from the topic. He leaned forward, arms resting on his knees. 'What kind of funding problems?'

'The usual kind, start-up money, unless a backer will help in the beginning. Later, of course, we expect it to pay for itself.' She paused, then said, 'I'm sure you're not interested in the problem.'

'Oh, but I am. Perhaps I can help.'

'How could you help?'

She probably pictured him, or anyone

connected with skydiving for that matter, about as far removed from knowing how to fund an opera as one could get without leaving the planet entirely.

'I have a few connections,' he went on, straightening in his chair and tipping it back, catching the underside of hers with one black-booted foot, as if imprisoning her between chair and desk. 'Have you ever heard of George Thomas Manning?'

She paused a moment. 'The name sounds familiar.'

'He's the richest man in the valley. And also, he's a member of the Society for the Arts.'

'Of course, *that* George Thomas Manning. You know him?' She looked surprised.

'I once worked for him.'

'As — ' she prompted.

'General flunky,' he said. 'Nevertheless, I think I know him pretty well. I have a feeling your opera thing would appeal to him. At any rate, you ought to try.'

'I will. I'll write to him as soon as — '

'No,' Colin interrupted, 'go to see him in person. Believe me, that will have the best results. Do it right away, today.'

She stood then, forcing him to move his legs or create a strong impression that she was his captive.

'You seem very anxious,' she said, walking to the wide office window, frowning slightly. 'It almost sounds as if you're trying to get rid of me.'

He could understand her having that feeling, one that didn't gibe with his asking for her just the day before. He rose quickly, his chair banging on the floor. 'You're very suspicious. I'm just trying to do a favor, make up a little for the way I treated you before. If my suggesting Manning's name helps you out, that doesn't mean I want you to quit our promotion. Can't you do both?'

She turned and studied his face. 'Not at the same time.'

'Well, then,' he continued, 'you can

do mine first and the opera thing later.'

She smiled, maybe considering that wasn't such a bad idea. Was it possible that, in spite of her fear of heights, she wanted to do his promotion, wanted to learn why he loved airplanes and why he jumped out of them? No, not just him, why anybody did. Could something about it have hooked her already?

'Perhaps.' she said. 'Thanks for telling me.'

'You're welcome. You will go to see him then, today?'

'Yes, I will see him, but only if we finish here first. If you keep changing the subject, we'll *never* get done.'

He laughed. 'Agreed. What do I do now, teacher?'

She pulled her pocket calendar from her purse and sat down again, and for the next hour, they pencilled in dates and places for his exhibition jumps and discussed the logistics of other skydivers, airplanes and airport clearances.

6

George Thomas Manning didn't live in Stafford, but in the country. The drive took Jennifer through the rolling hills, already turning gold, their summer color, dotted with deep green trees. Pink and white oleanders in the highway dividers added more color, and contrasted with the occasional deep purple of a flowering plum tree. Only peripherally aware of the beauty of the summer afternoon, she rehearsed what she'd say to Mr. Manning, how she'd urge him to sponsor the opera program, what it would mean to the community.

She thought of Colin's encouragement. How ironic that his suggestion might be the means to her end. She would have what she wanted, and, if she held Peter to his promise, could also be rid of the skydiving promotion. Colin's pleasant attitude during the past hour and her reluctant, but growing, interest in his sport hadn't completely dispelled her feeling that her attraction to him might be dangerous. She needed a complication like that in her life like a case of poison oak.

Almost an hour later, she slowed the speed of her aging compact and turned off the main highway onto a side road, then Manning Drive. Now that was the ultimate test of wealth, when people named streets after you.

But Manning Drive held few houses and even those were so widely spaced that she literally couldn't see two of them at the same time. When she reached a fork in the road, a sign on the left read, 'Manning Circle — Not a Through Street.'

Turning between the stone gates, Jennifer proceeded up the steep hill, suddenly besieged with doubts. What if he had gone somewhere today? What if he were too busy to see her? Because of Colin's urging, she hadn't phoned ahead for an appointment. How impetuous she'd been to simply jump in the car and drive there. Usually she was much more organized and practical. She couldn't back down now, but her palms were moist on the steering wheel of the car, and she felt a loose strand of hair cling to the nape of her neck.

All at once, the house came into view, a three-storied mansion, ivy clinging to its grey stone sides. It stood at the top of a rise, its lawn like a velvet carpet. A garage for five cars, with a second floor above it, flanked a greenhouse, its whitewashed panes reflecting the sun.

The driveway wound through trees and Jennifer occasionally lost sight of the house. Her attention suddenly catapulted back to the road when a small red sports car appeared directly in her path. She reacted instantly, yanking the steering wheel sharply to the right and going off the road onto the grassy bank. Her breathing almost stopped, her throat tightened.

As the sports car zoomed past, she glimpsed the other driver, a girl, and even in that split second Jennifer saw a pale face framed by jet-black hair. The car sped away, and Jennifer maneuvered back onto the drive again, mentally consigning people who drove too fast and on the wrong side of the road to reincarnation as snails. Then the gravel driveway crunched under her tires and she stopped in front of the solid oak door of the mansion. A butler opened it.

'I'm Jennifer Gray,' she said, handing him a business card. 'I'd like to see Mr. Manning.'

After leaving her briefly, he ushered her through a large hallway with a polished black and white terrazzo floor, then into a beautiful living room. Ceiling to floor mullioned windows flooded the room with light, revealing panelled walls, antique furniture, a huge marble-topped fireplace with a painted landscape above it and, in a chair nearby, an elderly, white-haired man, wearing a dark red jacket with black satin lapels.

Surprisingly agile for his years, the man came out of the chair quickly, crossed to her and shook her hand with a firm, though thin and bony, grip. In spite of his apparent advanced age, his face was smooth and handsome.

'Thank you for seeing me.'

'You were lucky to find me in — otherwise you'd have wasted your time driving up here. But, then, time is something you young people squander. When you have as little left as I do, you treat it with more respect.'

Jennifer paused to recover, wondering what bugged the old curmudgeon besides impatience. He looked pretty spry, so it probably wasn't ill health. Was it just general old age crankiness? She sat in the chair opposite him despite his not asking her to. She didn't plan to walk away until she had accomplished her mission.

'I've come to ask for your help,' she said.

'Do you realize, young lady, that anyone with two nickels to rub together is constantly bombarded with requests for help — they really mean money — and if we gave all of it away, we'd have nothing left and everyone else in the world would only be about two dollars richer?'

It was obviously a speech Manning had made before, and one he enjoyed, if only for the startled reaction he probably got in return. Okay, so she ought to feel ashamed of herself for doing the same thing. But she didn't intend to leave without a fight for her cause. She ignored his outburst and spoke up. 'I understand that you're a member of the Society for the Arts.'

He sat down opposite her. 'I founded that organization almost fifty years ago. What about it?'

Apparently proud of that accomplishment, he seemed to soften somewhat, almost smiled. Encouraged, she added, 'It's done a great deal of good. The list of its activities would fill a book. That's why I thought you might be willing to consider aid to an opera promotion.'

With only a pause to catch her breath, she went on, anxious to say as much as possible on its behalf before he could come up with any arguments. 'We've never had an opera in the valley. You have to go all the way to Los Angeles or San Francisco to see one.'

'There have been operettas — '

'Musical comedies, really, and not by professionals. The high schools do them, and East Valley College puts on a very nice show every year, but for the kind of production we want, we need a real opera company, and I have one lined up. We even have an auditorium back in Stafford that can be converted into an opera house with very little effort. All we need is a sponsor to underwrite the cost and guarantee the salaries for the company. But I'm sure it would pay for itself once it got started.'

She paused finally, catching her breath in the process.

The man narrowed his eyes and

looked her over before he spoke. 'Tell me more about it over tea.' He reached to the pie-crust edged table at his side and rang a silver bell.

Jennifer almost fainted with surprise. That was definitely an encouraging sign. 'Thanks, I'd love to.'

As they spoke, an hour flew by. While they drank tea and ate from a tray of tiny sandwiches, petit fours, and fresh fruit brought in by the butler, Manning warmed and opened, listening attentively to everything Jennifer had to say. He also explained the mystery of his sudden change in manner. It turned out his late wife had been the consummate opera devotee, so that, whereas some other request might have bought her a hasty rush to the door, the promise of an opera company met with his approval. He asked question after question, even wanted to know about her personal background.

Finally, aware she'd been doing most of the talking, she apologized. 'I'm sorry, I seem to be monopolizing the conversation.'

'Not at all. I've never been known for my reticence, and I'd like listening to you even if you weren't as pretty and charming as you are.'

Jennifer smiled at the compliment, then wondered, fleetingly, if the dark-haired girl she had noticed behind the wheel of the sports car had been visiting Mr. Manning.

'I'm also very impressed,' he went on, 'with your project and the preliminary work you've done.'

'Then you will help? You'll persuade the Society for the Arts to give us their backing?'

'I'll do more than that. If they don't agree, I'll finance the project myself.'

Jennifer almost leaped from her chair. 'Thank you very much. I can hardly wait to tell Mr. Cramden.' Excited about her success, she could hardly think. 'As soon as I find someone to handle the promotion I'm doing now — '

'And that is — ?' Manning asked, getting up to walk her to the hall.

'Oh, you'll laugh. It's a skydiving promotion. You know, where people actually put on parachutes and jump out of airplanes.'

'Skydiving?' His mood turned a hundred and eighty degrees again, and he almost snorted the word. 'My son is a skydiver. I haven't seen him for years.'

She frowned. She'd said the wrong thing.

'He didn't want to come into the family business,' Manning continued. 'That wasn't exciting enough for him.' He paused, as if realizing he had been momentarily carried away. 'Of course he was young, but — ' He looked up at Jennifer. 'He's a very good skydiver, though, so you may know him.'

Her voice cracked slightly. 'I've only met one so far and his name isn't Manning.'

'He hasn't been using my name. He dropped the Manning, whether from shame, or fear of embarrassing me, I don't know. He calls himself Colin Thomas.'

Jennifer felt the room spinning. Colin Thomas was his son? She looked into the old man's face and suddenly the resemblance between the two became startlingly apparent. The same blue eyes, the same perfect nose, the same lips that could be brought into a thin, hard line at times, the same firm chin that thrust forward, as if daring life to defeat any plans he might make.

'Yes, I know him,' she said, her voice barely more than a whisper. Colin had pulled another surprise out of his bag of tricks.

'Well, don't tell him you saw me. We had some bitter quarrels. I haven't forgiven him for that. I was already middle-aged when he was born, you see, and I expected him to take over my enterprises. When his mother died, he — '

Manning suddenly stopped, as if realizing he was telling private family history to an almost total stranger. He reached out and touched Jennifer's hand and abruptly changed the subject, his voice rising in pitch. 'I'll call you when the funding is all arranged.'

'You can reach me at the office. I'd be so grateful.' She handed him a business card, still unable to understand why Colin had sent her there, to his estranged father. She followed the butler back to the front door, climbed into her car, and drove away.

So he hated skydiving. Or at least he hated his son for taking up the sport. But, surely he should understand that people can't be forced into doing what they don't like. It wasn't as if Colin had become a criminal or a drug addict. He owned his own business, after all, and probably, considering the old man's attitude, had done it without a cent of help. He ought to be proud of his son instead of so belligerent. Then she thought of her own attitude about skydiving. Who was she to condemn his father on that score? Didn't she act just as intolerant about it? She had already written Colin off as a person whose life-style was completely abhorrent to her. Did she sound as unbending as Mr. Manning? Maybe so, but her reason was very different.

7

When she met Colin at the airport early Saturday morning, Jennifer saw that he drove one of the original Thunderbirds, a small, dark blue convertible that had obviously been restored with care. She hadn't intended to drive to Riverdale with him, but he had insisted that she would get lost otherwise, and besides, it seemed foolish and wasteful to drive two cars to the same place. She settled into the seat beside him, wondering how to broach the subject uppermost in her mind.

At her taping session that week, reading books into the microphone to record them for blind students, her thoughts had wandered many times to Colin. For one thing, there was the obvious physical attraction. But she also pondered his motive in ignoring his father for years, and then suddenly sending her to him. But the moment to ask him had arrived. They'd be alone for several hours.

She smoothed the jacket of her pant-suit into place, then tied a matching scarf over the hair she had not pinned up that day. 'I met your Mr. Manning.'

'Did you like him? Did he like you?'

Jennifer flashed a look at him. She had not expected that reaction. 'As a matter of fact, yes. That is, I think he likes me, not that it's a necessary ingredient for my promotion.'

'I could predict it. We have similar tastes in women.'

'You ought to, since he's your father.' She hadn't intended to sound quite so harsh, but somehow it had come out that way.

He glanced quickly at her, then his eyes returned to the road, but his jaw seemed tighter.

'So he told you, did he?'

'It came up, yes. I think you intended it to.'

'Perhaps.' The word was clipped.

'In that case, why didn't you tell me yourself?'

'Because if you'd mentioned I sent you, he'd have slammed the door in your face.' After a pause, he went on. 'I didn't think it was my place. I doubted whether he wanted to acknowledge me as his son — the black sheep of the family and all that — '

'What was so terrible about wanting to do your own thing?' Again Jennifer regretted her frankness. She was treading where she had no business.

But Colin answered. 'You don't understand. I committed the unforgivable sin. I refused to go into the family business.'

'I realize your father is elderly, but I didn't think anyone disinherited an unruly son anymore.'

Colin opened and closed his mouth twice before answering. 'I don't want to talk about it. Let's change the subject.'

'But you opened the subject by sending me to him.'

'Then I made a mistake. I thought I did you a favor.'

Jennifer had to admit she stood to gain much and he little, unless he wanted to be rid of her, which, considering his compliments and kissing her, didn't make sense. 'But you could at least try to reconcile with him. He is your father, after all.'

'Reconcile? I'm the one who calls and visits. Martin the butler should be my father. At least I get to see him.'

Jennifer was stunned. Was the old man really that unbending? 'I'm sorry.'

'It's okay. I shouldn't have sent you there. My intention was to help you, not open a hornet's nest. Let's not talk about it any more.'

The silence stretched for several miles while she tried to think of something helpful.

'Did you do your homework?' Colin asked finally.

'Homework? What homework?'

'Reading about skydiving, of course. Tell me, what's an altimeter?'

Grateful for the end of the uncomfortable silence, she cleared her throat and attempted an answer. 'It's a gauge, sort of. It tells how high you are off the ground.'

'Very good. Not exactly the way I would have phrased it, but acceptable. I'm impressed. What about a ripcord?'

'That's the thing you pull to make the parachute open.' She couldn't help smiling at herself, but her pleasure ended when he asked more technical questions. He had to answer those himself, then explained the day's events at Riverdale. Time flew by as fast as the landscape.

The town consisted of small stucco houses in pastel colors, but Colin didn't stop until they reached the air field well past the residential area. There, surrounded by distant green and gold hills, a large open meadow, crisscrossed in part by landing strips, was lined on one side by an apparently recently-constructed set of bleachers. A colorful canopy covered the structure and flags flew from the tops of the small buildings nearby. On the field sat three small planes and one large one.

Spectators arrived, parked their cars in the dirt at the edge of the field and walked leisurely to the bleachers, where they chose their seats. An enterprising vendor hawked his wares — hot dogs and soft drinks — and a young man with a wheeled cart sold ice cream.

Colin and Jennifer went directly to the hangar. Several other skydivers stood or sat around, along with an assortment of girl friends, pilots, mechanics, and some youngsters who were obviously fascinated by anything to do with airplanes.

Having finished with the publicity for the event, Jennifer had only to be sure the *Riverdale Herald* photographer took pictures, and that it all came off as printed in the programs. The event had actually been planned by one of the many California skydiving clubs: a target contest, where each man would jump from the same altitude and attempt to land on a yellow disc three inches in diameter. The admission charge would benefit the charity which had asked Piedmont Productions to organize the tour, and the skydivers donated their time and talents. They would have been jumping on a fine Saturday afternoon anyway — a victory cup or second place ribbons constituted their prizes.

Jennifer took in the sights and sounds of the sport. The talk seemed almost exclusively concerned with wind conditions, which she didn't understand. All of the men — no women skydivers participated that particular day — wore colorful jumpsuits made of a nylon-like material. They fit snugly at neck, wrist and ankles and sported numerous zippered pockets. Helmets and gloves completed the costume, and, for the moment at least, their parachutes rested on a large table in the corner. Someone had brought a pot of coffee and all helped themselves to it, using Styrofoam cups, but no one ate, although it was past noon and Jennifer, at least, was starting to get hungry.

Colin pulled his blue jumpsuit over his street clothes and introduced Jennifer to the others. She tried to remember all their names, but in their jumpsuits and helmets, they all tended to look alike.

'This is Mike Drummond,' Colin said. 'He's the president of the Riverdale Skydiving Club.'

Jennifer shook hands with the tall, slender young man whose brown hair waved back from a high forehead.

'Glad to meet you.' He squeezed her hand in a firm grip. 'I hear you're the P.R. person for this whole tour of Colin's. Sounds like a big responsibility. And you've done a good job today. There are certainly a lot more people here than I would have expected.'

She smiled. 'We hope to raise a large amount for charity.'

He excused himself. 'I have a few more things to do. Starting time is one o'clock.'

‘Find a good seat where you can watch,’ Colin told her.

‘I suppose I should, but first I think I’ll patronize that vendor and get something to eat. I’m famished. Aren’t you going to eat something too?’

‘No, most skydivers don’t eat just before jumping.’

‘I once read that bullfighters don’t eat beforehand just in case they’re gored and need a quick operation.’

Colin’s face took on a puzzled look and then he laughed. ‘You read too much.’

‘I beg your pardon?’

‘There’s very little similarity between skydiving and bullfighting,’ he continued. ‘We have no adversary up there except ourselves, and if an accident occurs, no surgeon in the world will be able to put us back together again, lunch or no lunch.’

‘I’m sorry,’ she said, ‘I didn’t mean — ’

‘It’s all right. It’s what we love to do and we don’t think it’s very dangerous

— although sometimes we like the public to think it is — but we never lose sight of the fact that stupidity and carelessness can cause accidents. Maybe we don't eat before a jump because we're nervous.'

'No one looks nervous. You all look so completely relaxed and carefree.'

'Oh, we're nervous all right, but don't tell anyone I said that.' He smiled and gave her a wink.

Jennifer suddenly lost her hunger, and she too became nervous, for him, for all the men who defied death every Saturday afternoon with only a bolt of Dacron for protection.

'I'm beginning to think I shouldn't have come along after all,' she said. 'What if someone — ' She stopped.

'Hey, wait a minute, don't even think it. Nothing's going to happen. Being nervous is just part of the routine. It happens to everyone in sports: the downhill skier just before he pushes off, or the race-car driver in the pit before the flag drops. That's what it's all about.'

'But this is dangerous. What if the 'chute doesn't open?'

'The chances of even one parachute not opening are about one in ten thousand, and we wear two of them. What do you suppose the chances are of both of them not opening?'

'Pretty high, I guess.'

'Right. Besides, we pack our own. And professional packers do the reserve. And I could tell you stories about guys who fell with *no* parachute and lived to fly again.'

'Really?' She tried to be reassured, and the touch of his hands comforted her, but as the tension mounted in the hangar — as the men began to put on their chutes — she found she couldn't erase the fluttering feelings inside.

'Go on out now,' Colin urged, fastening on his own parachute.

Jennifer followed another girl to a ladder at the side of a building and climbed to the flat roof which gave a superb view of the field, its target circle and the plane taxiing to the runway. In a few moments the boys who had been in the hangar and some of the girlfriends of other skydivers joined them.

A hot afternoon sun beating down on them, they watched the converted C-47 getting into position, a door on one side conveniently removed. Then the twelve skydivers walked out to the field, to the shouts and applause of the crowd, and entered the plane. It roared off into a cloudless sky. A hush fell over everyone, even the vendors stopped trying to sell popcorn. Necks craning, heads tilted upward, all watched the plane become a tiny speck against the blue backdrop of the sky and seem to disappear. When it returned to their field of vision, someone called, 'Here he comes,' and Jennifer saw the first man leap from the open door of the plane and come falling to earth, arms and legs spread out and slightly bent at elbows and knees. He fell for what seemed an incredibly long time. She could see him clearly by the time he pulled his ripcord and the parachute billowed out above him, snapping him upward into a perpendicular position. Then began the test of his skill, as he maneuvered his chute in the air. Unlike the one she'd seen Colin use the week before, this one was colorful and almost square, like a quilted bed sheet in the wind. Lower and lower he came, and finally he touched down near the target, not directly on it, but close. Three striped-shirted judges announced his distance at only six centimeters. The crowd roared its approval, and the skydiver, pulling his chute down, hastily got out of the way of the next man, already close to the pit.

Several jumpers — all of them under similar square canopies — touched the edges of the disc, which seemed as close as anyone could come, but Jennifer had already heard of Colin's reputation as the best.

He had been the last man out of the plane and her pulse began to race as soon as she saw him in the air. Her neck aching from the strain of looking up, she watched him free fall, arms and legs outstretched, his blue jumpsuit almost matching the color of the sky around him, the darker color of the parachutes on his chest and back giving him a distorted outline.

'Pull the ripcord,' she told him mentally. 'You're too low, pull your ripcord!'

Seconds seemed to stretch into minutes, and she felt ready to burst from the tension. Then the chute popped out, and he pulled on the lines, sailing sideways through the sky, his head down, his gaze riveted on the target.

One foot raised and bent at the knee, the other landed dead center on the disc, driving it into the ground. The crowd screamed, people jumped up and down in the stands. Jennifer breathed again. He was safe.

And then a terrible thought came to her. Why was she so worried? Was she falling for him after all?

She sat still, barely aware of the others around her. Of course not. She could never fall in love with a skydiver. She had no intention of marrying young, like her mother. Twenty-nine, she'd decided, was a good age — after she'd established her career — so she had been very careful in her relationships with men. So far, no one, certainly not Colin Thomas, had come into her life who posed any threat to her plan.

Although she loved her mother dearly, she imitated her no further than her ready smile and desire to help others. Helen Rogers had married Christopher Gray right out of high school, giving birth to Jennifer before either of them was nineteen. Jennifer knew about the low-paying jobs her father had to take and vowed not to live like that. Unlike her parents, she made long-range plans. She had a degree and now a promising career.

Someday she'd marry, but only to

someone more like herself. Her plan never included a skydiver. Their hedonistic life-style, hanging around airports, jumping out of planes, contributed little to society. Until this promotion came along and she put some of them to work for charity.

But what about Colin? For a moment she thought only of the handsome face, the intelligence, the humor. No, the man was nothing but an irresponsible gypsy moth attracting crowds of impressionable young girls. True, he could be charming when it suited him, and actually apologized for his bad manners. And he didn't just jump out of airplanes — he owned a flying service — but he was so maddeningly . . . What?

Well, she argued with herself, which was it she most objected to, his life-style or his attention to her? Both. She objected to everything about him. Then why had she been so frightened for him? Because he was a human being — she cared about everyone.

But she had no sweaty palms when Mike Drummond jumped, or Sandy 'What's-his-name.' She shook her head violently. But she didn't even like him.

Sure, like she didn't like chocolate.

8

The plane went up again and again that afternoon. Each man was to have six jumps and their total score would determine the winner. Whereas none of the men, except Colin, had hit the disc dead center on the first try, they improved with practice and all of them did it by the third jump. Mike Drummond, whom Jennifer remembered meeting in the hangar, hit dead center on the second and every other jump until the sixth and then missed it by four centimeters, the same distance by which he had missed it the first time.

Colin, with five dead center landings, seemed assured of winning, so long as he landed no farther than seven centimeters on the last try. But this time his approach seemed off, and Jennifer tensed, hoping he would make it, but afraid he'd miss by just enough to lose the contest.

But, then, in the last few seconds, he maneuvered the parachute over the pit area, and his foot went down right on top of the disc. He had won the event.

The men lined up on the platform, and the judges awarded the prizes, to loud applause from the audience.

A noisy, happy crowd filled the small café where they all assembled for dinner that night. Huge platters of spaghetti, baskets of Italian bread, and bottles of wine covered the checkered tablecloths. There were about thirty people in the group, almost half of them young girls who looked up adoringly at their skydiver boy friends and hung on their every word. Jennifer sat between Colin and Mike and listened to the banter between them about coming in first and second again. Mike vowed he would beat Colin at it one day, and they talked about their jumps, how the wind had affected them, and many things about parachutes and skydiving that Jennifer didn't understand.

All around her, the men spoke of other events, other days, other people, and, surprisingly, she found all of the talk interesting, though she couldn't participate. Mike politely asked her about her promotion work and seemed genuinely interested in hearing about advertising copywriting and layouts. To Jennifer it had suddenly become terribly boring. Previously she had only compared her job with the office work of her friends, and by that yardstick hers held much more variety, but for excitement it could hardly compare to skydiving.

Colin tried to include her in the conversation, but, content to listen, she watched him, catching everyone's admiration for his skill and personality.

Near midnight they finally left the camaraderie of the café and headed back toward the cars, some couples pairing off, arms entwined. Jennifer followed Colin to the convertible and they sped off down the open highway.

'How did you like your first parachuting event?'

'I loved it,' she admitted. 'I had no idea it would be so exciting and yet controlled. Of course, you told me in advance about the competition and the judges and all that, but somehow, seeing it firsthand is very different.'

'Are you ready to admit we're not a bunch of crackpots?'

'If so, you're the nicest bunch of crackpots I ever met. And, after seeing so many jumps in one afternoon, I've almost begun to take it for granted.'

'I told you it was safe.'

'Exciting, yes. Fun, yes. Safe it's not.'

'There's an old joke that goes, 'What's the most dangerous part of skydiving?' and the answer is, 'driving to the airport.' '

She laughed with him. 'Even after I got used to it, I still had a strange feeling when I saw you jump from the plane and you seemed to float in the air. Although I knew you'd open your parachute — '

'You were worried about me?'

She was glad the darkness kept him from seeing her face. 'I didn't mean you personally,' she amended. 'I meant any of the men.' She didn't care to admit even to herself that indeed he, personally, had concerned her, that she found herself thinking about him even when he was not in mid-air.

'What do *you* feel?' she went on, turning the tables. 'Do you enjoy the danger? Is that why you do it so much?'

'It's not dangerous, but it is exciting — at least — ' He didn't finish his sentence, but started another. 'Describing skydiving to someone who's never done it is a bit like trying to explain television to King Arthur.'

'What do you do when you're not jumping?' she asked next. 'Just wait around impatiently for the next weekend?'

'Hardly. I work, you know. I teach both skydiving and flying.'

'Then you do spend all of your time

there, your own little world, so to speak?'

'You make it sound provincial,' he said. 'I assure you I know what's going on in the world. My awareness extends a lot further than the distance between plane and earth.'

'Still, you are somewhat — well, isolated — aren't you, from what happens in the real world?'

'It depends on what you mean by 'real,' doesn't it?'

'Well, don't most people manage a normal career and hobbies at the same time?'

'You haven't even asked me what my hobbies are. Some people might have skydiving for a hobby. But that's my business. My hobby is running an aviation service.' He grinned at her.

'I'm only trying to understand what fascinates you so that you spend your entire life — '

'Some people,' Colin answered, cutting her off, 'would think my father's world is real, running Manning Enterprises from behind a desk. I couldn't spend my entire life doing that.'

'Is running Skyway Aviation so different from running Manning Enterprises?'

He turned his head to her, stared at her face for some seconds and said, 'I'd rather not talk about it.'

She wondered if she had hit a nerve. He had started his rebellion from his father purely by skydiving and now he had a business which probably entailed some of the same sorts of problems he'd run away from.

'Well,' she said, 'I seem to have a knack for bringing up subjects you can't discuss.'

Colin lifted his right hand from the steering wheel and covered Jennifer's where it lay on the seat between them. Its strong touch sent a wave of warmth through her.

'It's not your fault,' he said. 'It's mine.'

'No, you were quite right. Your life-style is your own affair. I shouldn't have pried — '

'Your curiosity is normal, in fact, flattering, and, as you said earlier today, I rather invited it by telling you about my father. I think it must mean that I want to confide in you, to get to know you very well.' He squeezed her hand.

She pulled it away. He could confide all he wanted to, but they were not going to get to know one another as well as he might be hoping. She'd already decided that fortune tellers would find no skydivers in *her* tea leaves, even one who made her feel very comfortable and desirable. And had a great sense of humor besides.

'I think it's time we did change the subject,' she said, keeping her inflection light and breezy. 'We could talk about the weather. Oh, excuse me,' and she gave a little laugh, 'that would be shop talk for you, wouldn't it? Well, then, how about books or music or the theater?'

'Those are your fields, aren't they?' he asked, his tone equally bantering.

'You'd like to put me at a disadvantage — '

He stopped in mid-sentence and at the same moment Jennifer wondered if there was something wrong with the car. It was too warm for this time of night, and as he slowed the Thunderbird, she saw steam rise from the hood.

'What's the matter?'

Without answering, Colin slowed still more, pulled off onto the side of the road and stopped the car. White clouds filled the black sky in front of them. He released his seat belt and got out, then took his gloves out of his duffle bag in the back seat before attempting to raise the hood. When he did, still more steam poured out.

She looked around. Talk about your middle of nowhere. All she could see were miles of open fields — they had been driving through farm country. No filling stations, not even a house loomed on the horizon.

She got out of the car and went around to stand near him while he peered into the engine compartment as well as he could.

'Broken hose,' he told her. 'At least I think that's all it is. I can't really tell.'

'What will you do?' She hoped he had something in mind other than walking to an all-night station which — if there were such a thing — might be umpteen miles away. In what direction?

'Nothing.'

'Nothing?' She accompanied the word with wide-open eyes and a direct stare into his face. This was not the something she hoped he'd come up with.

'Look, we're on the proverbial deserted road — I can't remember when we passed another car — it's dark and I'm tired. Besides I never let anyone else tinker with my car. By morning it will have cooled off and I'll fix it. I always do.'

'Morning?' She felt like a parrot, repeating his words, but nothing more sensible came to her that didn't involve some display of outrage. And what was there to be outraged about? It wasn't his fault the car chose to break down in this particular forsaken spot. With the abundance of steam that had come from the vehicle, she could hardly suggest it was a variation on the old 'I've run out of gas' routine.

Then she was aware he had gone around to the back of the car and opened the trunk, the same place he kept his parachutes.

She tried for a flip comment, something that showed him she wasn't one of those panicky women who had hysterics when things didn't go well. 'You don't happen to have a hot-air balloon in there too, do you?'

'No, but I have two sleeping bags.'

She bit her lip rather than repeat the words again, but that didn't mean she didn't want very much to do so.

'There's a cornfield right here that looks downright cozy. I don't know about you, but I am much too tired to do anything but catch a few hours sleep.' He slammed the trunk lid.

He was serious.

'Come on,' he urged, 'try camping out. You might like it.' He threaded his way through rows of cornstalks that were as high as his waist.

Before he disappeared completely out of sight, she grabbed the other sleeping bag, and, dragging it behind her, followed his trail. 'My idea of camping out,' she called after him, 'is a second-class hotel.'

She heard his deep laugh. 'In that case, I'll downgrade my offer to 'roughing it.' Be a little unconventional, just once.'

Unconventional it would be, then. She was no hot-house flower, and besides, she knew when she was licked.

After a few minutes they found themselves in an open space about ten feet square among the stalks and Colin spread out a tarpaulin, which he had also carried from the car, and then unzipped his sleeping bag and spread it out.

'If we unzip both bags,' he suggested, 'we can spread one out on the tarp for a mattress, and then put the other over us as a blanket.'

'I don't think so.' She put her own bag as far away from his as the opening in the field would allow. 'We'll sleep separately if you don't mind.'

'I was only trying to help,' he said, pretending to be wounded by her assumptions. 'It would be warmer that way.'

'I don't think we need to be concerned about warmth.' His playfulness amused her. 'In fact, it's far too warm even for sleeping bags,' and with that she opened hers flat too, slipped off her sandals and jacket, and lay down without any covering, savoring the warm, balmy air. She looked up at the sky. 'What a beautiful night.'

'Yep. Stars and everything.'

She continued to stare, fascinated by the deep blackness of the night and the millions of stars, so bright they seemed near enough to touch. She breathed deeply, then sniffed. 'What's that?'

'Nothing much, just a skunk. Don't tell me you've never smelled a skunk before.'

'I think I've smelled that odor before, but I didn't know skunks made it.'

'My dear young lady,' Colin said, in mock seriousness, 'you may know all there is about music, books and drama, but it's time you learned something about the 'real world.' '

'Touché,' she said.

'In fact, isn't that a skunk over there?' He propped himself on one elbow and pointed with his free hand. 'There. That black furry thing with the white stripe.'

She stared into the cornstalks where he pointed, but saw nothing. He was probably teasing her. Nevertheless, she pulled her sleeping bag closer to his.

Aware of his very disturbing presence next to her, she didn't feel tired anymore. Instead her blood raced in her veins, her body poised as if for some adventure, and sleep the furthest thing from her mind. She closed her eyes tightly to squeeze out even the peripheral vision of him, but they refused to stay shut, springing open like twin Jack-in-the-Boxes. She explored the heavens, searching for the constellations she remembered from school days, and found the Big Dipper.

Suddenly his warm breath brushed her cheek. 'I have a confession to make,' he said in a soft, low voice.

'What is it?' She, too, spoke softly.

'I'm not sorry the car broke down. If it hadn't I probably wouldn't be spending the night with you.'

'You make it sound like — '

She didn't finish the sentence because his mouth was over hers, with a kiss that was as soft as a feather. He raised his face again, looking intently into her eyes. She lay still, waiting — yes, waiting, she forced herself to admit — for him to kiss her again, for that exquisite moment to be repeated. It had been too short. Her mouth yearned for his, and her body ached with the need to feel his warm touch.

As if in complete understanding and response, his lips, before so tender, came forcefully this time, his mouth firm with pressure, searching for the return of his kiss. Her arms went instinctively around his neck and she held him to her. She felt his arms go around her back, raising her from the ground and crushing her to him.

Her body responded to every sweet sensation, as if she could feel each nerve ending individually and reveled in its aliveness. His moist lips left hers and kissed her cheeks, her eyelids, her throat. His husky voice left soft words in her hair.

Then, like a bubble bursting, her ecstacy evaporated. Her throat tightened and cold reality came flooding in on her. What possessed her, letting him kiss her that way, this man whom she disliked just two weeks ago, who, even now, she would never consciously choose for herself?

She pulled away and pushed against his chest. 'Please,' she said, her mouth suddenly dry. 'Please stop.'

He looked into her face, questioning her sudden withdrawal. 'I'm only — ' he began, but she cut off his words, suddenly angry with herself for having succumbed to those wild emotions. How could she have let that happen?

'You only want to make love to me,' she said, struggling from his embrace, breathing heavily.

'I'm attracted to you,' he said. 'I don't think that's any secret. And you seemed to be enjoying yourself.'

'You wanted to add another conquest to your list. Admit it. Well, I won't be one of your 'groupies.' ' She tried to rise from the makeshift bed.

Colin, sitting upright beside her, shoved her back down on the sleeping bag. 'Lie still,' he demanded, 'and listen to me. I admit only to being caught up in the moment. I lost my head. As did you,' he added.

She couldn't speak.

His eyes had turned to bluish-green and glowed like cats' eyes in the dark. 'I never planned to make love to you, certainly not against your will. I don't need a string of conquests to prove anything. I know who and what I am. And I suggest you think about that yourself. I didn't find you exactly unwilling a moment ago.'

He paused to catch his breath. 'You'd better decide precisely how you feel before you accuse me of having designs on your body. In other words, Miss Gray, reserve your maidenly protests for when you're asked!'

With that he snatched his sleeping bag from her side and moved it as far away as the wall of cornstalks would allow, then threw himself on it, and turned his back to her.

She stared at his withdrawn form, feeling confused, humiliated and ashamed. For what seemed hours, she stared into the sky, feeling a complete fool. He was right, of course. She shouldn't have assumed he would try to make love to her. And if he did, hadn't she invited it by her own actions?

She lay still in the dark, listening to the sounds of crickets and an occasional truck rumbling somewhere in the far distance, still feeling the touch of his lips on hers. She had determined not to let herself be carried away by his good looks, charm and glamorous occupation. Yet, she had succumbed, like a child at a carnival. But knowing the danger, she would never let it happen again. Nevertheless, hot tears escaped from under her eyelids and slid like boiling rivers across her cheeks.

Much later, she drifted into sleep and in her dreams she saw a dark-haired man, who looked very much like Colin Thomas, come up the walk of a vine-covered cottage. He wore a jumpsuit over business clothes, carried a brief case in one hand and a ripcord in the other, and a helmet shone on his head. Not a skydiving helmet, but a silver visored one, the kind worn by knights.

9

Colin lay awake longer than Jennifer, heard her ragged breathing gradually become relaxed and rhythmic. When his own physical turmoil subsided, he quietly brought his sleeping bag closer and watched the rise and fall of her breasts as she slept.

God, she was desirable! And found him so too, if her momentary passion could be believed. What a fine kettle of fish this had turned into. They still had five more shows to get through. How could he keep his hands off her that long? There was obviously a fire there. It seemed only a matter of time before it burst into a roaring blaze.

He carefully lifted a strand of silky hair from her cheek. What if he slowed down, really got to know her better? Perhaps then he wouldn't want her to go out of his life as every other woman he knew had done, pushed aside when they no longer suited each other. But was that what he really wanted?

* * *

Jennifer thought she must still be dreaming when she first heard loud banging. She opened her eyes to bright daylight flooding in on her, and the sound of tools on metal. Standing up in the cornfield, she looked toward the road and saw the hood of the Thunderbird pointing skyward, and Colin's form hunched under it. Her watch confirmed that it was well into morning.

But what about last night? She had a vivid memory of being kissed as she never had before. Or was that part of the dream, the dream with the knight?

Wait, there was more. She had quarreled with the knight, said something awful to him. In a flash the scene came alive again, and she felt the same embarrassment. Okay, so it happened.

What should she do about it, pretend it didn't? Act as if they were still the same friends they'd been moments before that kiss? Confront him? Apologize?

Those were the alternatives. They didn't include standing in a cornfield all day. Face it. Get it over with.

After smoothing her clothes as best she could and pulling her comb through her tangled hair, she rolled up her sleeping bag, folded the tarp it lay on, and dragged the remains of her bed through the field.

At her approach, he lifted his head. 'Good morning. Sleep well?'

Good grief, he was jolly. He wanted to forget the night before as much as she did. She thanked him mentally and tried to put on a smile. Except that the inside of her mouth felt like an old tennis ball and she thought seriously of swapping a year of her life for a tall glass of cold orange juice. If anyone would ask her. Instead she just said a simple, 'Hello,' and then dumped her load into the trunk of the car.

'You're just in time,' he said, moving to the side of the car and then sliding smoothly underneath it. 'You can hand me tools when I ask for them.'

Oh, sure, like she would know one tool from another. But, anything to get the car repaired so she could get home and take a hot shower. She felt as if every pore was filled with dirt and straw and her guilty conscience made a black 'F' for 'Fool' on her forehead.

'Whatever you say.' She tried to sound cheerful.

After a moment, he waved his arm and his muffled voice asked for something. Since there was a collection of shiny tools lying on a square of black leather nearby, she assumed he wanted one of those and picked up a long skinny one and slapped it into his hand like nurses did for doctors in all those movies.

'No, not that one.'

She tried another, and then another and eventually he used one of them to make some more noise, squirmed out from under the car, checked something under the hood again, and finally climbed into the driver's seat and started the engine.

'It's all fixed,' he announced. 'At least, long enough to get us back to town.'

He wore the smile of someone very pleased with himself, as if he had just conquered Everest, but it was endearing, too, and since he was also acting like Sir Galahad about the night before, she only smiled and got in beside him.

At the first restaurant they saw, he stopped and they had a light breakfast, and Colin teased her about her 'adventure.'

'I may turn you into an outdoors person yet,' he joked.

'Not until they install color television and VCR's in every pup-tent,' she joked back.

But, as they headed toward the city again, the scene in the cornfield continued to play itself in Jennifer's head like an old commercial jingle. Why was he so darned pleasant this morning? Was his anger really gone?

Perhaps she should apologize now. 'About last night — ' she began.

But he cut her short. 'Last night should never have happened. I didn't plan it.'

'I know you didn't. We were both — carried away. I shouldn't have accused you — '

'The truth is you *should* accuse me. No,' he added hastily, 'I didn't fake the car trouble. Not unless I can do things like that subconsciously. With any other woman, I'd have suggested a stop at a motel when we left the restaurant last night, but with you . . . ' He left the sentence unfinished.

'We haven't known each other very long,' she offered.

'It's not that. I'm afraid too many young women have flung themselves at me. Regardless of your opinion, skydiving is very glamorous to most females. A skydiver is an automatic hero to them. But you're different. It didn't excite or interest you.'

A gnawing guilt swept through her. Skydiving had seemed stupid to her at first, but now everything had changed. She loved what she had seen the day before.

'I must apologize,' she began.

He interrupted. 'Don't! I guess I'm just ornery enough to like you the way you are.' He gave her a tender look before returning his gaze to the road. 'So I'm not a hero to you, so what? I do have some other qualities, some you may actually care for. And I'll still want to kiss you in the moonlight.'

He placed his arm around her shoulders and pulled her closer. Confused thoughts swirled in her head. Suddenly she felt sixteen again and having her first date with a boy. But teenage dates didn't mean anything — they were not commitments for the future. Colin's surprising speech indicated he intended to pursue his interest. If she accepted his attentions, he might think she could be serious about him, too, and she couldn't. No longer a teenager, her life plan didn't include him. It would be cruel to lead him on and let him think that it did.

She remembered the night before and how she succumbed momentarily to a sudden desire for the man. This morning, she knew she had to continue to do her job, work with him and still not become involved. It wouldn't be easy. But how could she tell him without antagonizing him, perhaps jeopardizing the harmony of the tour?

Before she could even attempt to assemble her thoughts to reply, he turned on the car radio to a music station and began singing along, so Jennifer — for the moment at least — postponed the necessity of finding the right words to explain herself. His good humor was infectious and she joined in on songs she recognized.

When they arrived at the airport in Stafford, where she had left her own car, several people stood around the field in spite of the time and the day.

She had hoped for a few moments of privacy with Colin, unhindered by his driving and singing, but after the Thunderbird pulled into the parking area, and Colin climbed out, Whitey Franklin approached them.

'Hey,' he said, 'where have you two been?' and he grinned like a conspirator and punched a friendly fist into Colin's arm.

'Only to London for the changing of the guard,' Colin said.

Although everyone laughed, Jennifer felt her scalp tingle with embarrassment. Naturally they all assumed she and Colin had spent the night together, and not as innocently as it had turned out. But she knew that trying to explain would only make it seem worse, so she got out of the car without comment.

'I think I'll be going now.'

'I'll see you tomorrow.' Colin held her hand for a brief moment, then walked with her toward her own car. After she got in, and he closed the door for her, he walked away.

She slowly backed the car out of its

parking place, then drove toward the exit. Through the rear view mirror, she noticed that instead of walking back to his own car, Colin headed toward a tall, dark-haired girl she hadn't noticed before. The distance between them did nothing to hide the fact that she wore a lot of make-up, her black hair flowed glamorously around her shoulders, and a bright green dress emphasized her stunning figure.

As she unconsciously lifted her foot from the accelerator, Jennifer's car slowed to a stop, and she stared at the girl, who looked, somehow, familiar. Where had she seen that face before?

The girl threw her arms around Colin's neck and they hugged, after which she led him to a small red sports car.

And then Jennifer remembered where she had seen that face: on the way to the Manning house two weeks before. A dark-haired girl had been driving that red sports car on the wrong side of the road and forced Jennifer to swerve into the grass.

Her foot came down hard and the car leaped forward like a jackrabbit, then swerved into the street. So, all his talk about liking her the way she was had been just another line. He had a girlfriend, probably one of those teenagers to whom skydiving was the ultimate thrilling sport.

Jennifer's jaw tensed and her head began to throb.

She struggled to compose herself as she drove, but his deception galled her. Just when she had begun to think him as more than just a shallow opportunist, he spoiled it all by saying one thing and acting another.

An inner voice mocked her. Whoa, there. Why was she so upset? She didn't want the man herself, so this couldn't be jealousy, could it?

Of course not. Their relationship was strictly business, and that's the way she wanted it. The appearance of the beautiful brunette would actually simplify her task of keeping Colin in his place. She should be grateful, actually, that this had happened. It protected her from falling in love with the wrong man.

But then, why did she feel so disappointed?

10

Jennifer was considerably calmer on Monday morning, in spite of a nagging sensation whenever she thought of Colin. Should she be polite or distant, question him about the girl she'd seen hugging him or ignore it? Normally, she'd conclude it was none of her business, especially since she knew she didn't want to encourage him to pursue *her*. But, would he think it odd if she *didn't* comment?

Convincing herself she needed to work in the office, she pushed the dilemma aside temporarily and spent her morning making telephone calls, writing news releases and preparing sketches for posters for the upcoming exhibitions. By noon, she succumbed to the inevitable and headed for Skyway Aviation, but once there, she rationalized that she couldn't do any work on an empty stomach and walked to the A-frame building that served as the field's only restaurant. Whitey Franklin sat alone at a table, but jumped up at her approach and held a chair for her.

'Thanks. You're a real gentleman. It's seldom I have my chair held for me anymore.'

'I guess I just can't stop doing things the old way. No matter what the women's lib types think, I still like to treat women with respect. Especially pretty ones like yourself,' he added with a wink.

'Well, thank you again.'

'I may not be young anymore, but I still appreciate the finer things in life. You know the old saying, don't you? There may be snow on the roof, but there's still a fire in the furnace!' And he laughed as he pointed to his thatch of white hair and then to his heart.

After they ordered lunch, she asked Whitey if he had looked over her final plans for the drops. They had agreed in advance she would make them but he would double-check, since she lacked his experience with the procedures. That day, she was especially grateful for the arrangement, as it meant she might not have to see Colin at all. Then she could postpone deciding whether or not she should mention the brunette with the red sports car.

'Yes,' Whitey assured her. 'You did just fine. You even got all those pesky forms signed okay.'

'That's the worst part,' she said. 'I had no idea authorities required so much paperwork before they'd let someone do sport parachuting.'

'Gets worse every year,' he said. 'And you know, every year more people do it, and it keeps getting safer and more common, and yet every year someone else seems to want to get into the act and require another form that we aren't going to kill ourselves or someone else or damage somebody's property. Why, I remember when all I had to do was get permission from the pilot.'

'Did you used to jump, Whitey? I

didn't know that.'

'Yes, I was one of the first. Would you believe it, that was nearly forty years ago.'

'I had no idea people had been doing it that long.'

'Longer than that. Parachutes are older than airplanes.'

'You're not serious?' Jennifer looked at him skeptically.

'Seventeen ninety-seven.' He announced. 'They used to jump from hot air balloons.'

'Seventy ninety-seven? You certainly don't show your age.'

They both laughed, and then the waitress brought their food. After she'd gone, Whitey continued, interrupting his narrative with bites of his ham and swiss cheese sandwich. 'I meant in the United States. The sport started in France, and I learned from a Frenchman myself.'

'You don't mean Jacques Istel, do you?' Jennifer asked.

Whitey paused, his sandwich halfway

to his mouth. 'You know about Istel?'

'I came across his name in my reading about the sport.'

'I learned from another fellow, George something or other. Can you believe it? I've forgotten his last name. But I met Jacques Istel once. I lived in Phoenix — it was early '70's — and he came there to do a jump. Didn't look like a Frenchman to me. Too tall, I thought, where George was short and dark.'

'Did you jump with Istel?'

'Nope. He ran his own show.'

'I'll bet you've seen a lot of interesting things.'

'Yes, the sport sure has changed over the years though. Why, I remember when they had free fall contests to see how long you could fall before you opened your parachute, nothing any sane person would do today.'

'Why is that?'

'Well, how long you fall depends on your altitude when you jump, doesn't it?'

‘I guess so.’

‘And we all jumped from the same plane at the same height. And the other thing is when you open your ’chute.’

‘I see. You mean in order to win the contest you had to delay opening the parachute as long as possible — ’

‘Risk your neck, darn near kill yourself.’

She cringed at the thought of men seeing how close they could come to the ground before opening the parachute, like teenagers playing ‘chicken’ with automobiles on back roads. ‘Didn’t someone stop it?’

‘Oh, sure, the skydivers themselves. They regulated things, and made safety rules and they just stopped having contests like that. These days they do more landing on targets. I remember when they used huge pieces of white cloth for targets, laid on the ground in the shape of an ‘X’. Now the jumpers are so accurate they land on that little disc. And they have competitions to do certain stunts in the air, and make stars, like they're going to do at the lake. It's all a lot safer. I hate all that paperwork, but I'm sure glad they made some rules.'

'So am I. I wouldn't want to be involved with anything as risky as that. In fact, I almost didn't take this assignment because I thought the sport was too dangerous.'

'Like I've just been saying, it's not anymore. You ought to try it yourself.'

'Try skydiving?'

'Sure, why not?'

She hesitated about telling him of her fear of heights. It was bad enough that Colin knew. So she stalled. 'But in spite of these new safety rules, don't people still get killed?'

'People get killed driving cars too,' he said, 'but that doesn't stop anyone from doing it, 'cause they know that if they're one of the careful ones it won't happen to them.' He took a swallow of coffee. 'Same with skydiving. If you're one of the sensible ones, it's perfectly safe. Anyway, they say more people get hurt in their bathrooms and kitchens than anywhere else.'

'That's an interesting statistic,' she admitted, 'but I don't need a parachute if I slip on a banana peel.'

He laughed and took another bite of his sandwich.

Jennifer had always tried to be honest with herself, and she had to admit she'd begun to admire the sport. Spending so much time at the field, watching so many jumpers, it fascinated her, no longer seemed so scary. Even so, she knew she could never do it herself, not while she was still afraid of heights.

'You don't have to do an actual jump,' Whitey continued. 'You could just take the ground lessons. It would give you a good idea of the kind of training a jumper gets before he goes up for the first time.'

He had hit on the right motive: she had always believed in getting all the facts before tackling an assignment.

'I suppose I could do that,' she admitted. 'What's it like, a lot of lectures? How can you practice something you have to get right the first time?'

'Oh, you'd be surprised what you'd learn.' Then he added eagerly, 'There's a class just starting tomorrow. It goes for three days. You take that and you'll learn plenty. I guarantee you'll be a different woman.'

The only different person she wanted to be was someone who wasn't afraid of heights, and she didn't think ground school — if you never left the ground — would work, yet —

'I'll think about it. Where would I sign up?'

'You don't have to sign up anywhere. Just come to the office tomorrow afternoon at two o'clock. Wear a jumpsuit — you can buy new or second-hand equipment at the store on the other side of the field, you know — and I'll give you a book to read first.'

'I'll read the book, but I can't promise.'

'Believe me, it's not like the old days.

Sometimes I wonder how I stayed alive, jumping all those years ago, when they didn't have licensed instructors or jumpmasters or supervised competitions.'

'What's a jumpmaster?'

'The person in charge of every jump, just like it sounds. He's the boss, and no one does anything except what the jumpmaster tells him.'

'Is Colin a jumpmaster?' she asked, then wished she hadn't brought up his name. She didn't want Whitey, or anyone, to know the man occupied so much of her thoughts. And that she was making a considerable effort to fight her attraction to him.

'Oh, yes,' Whitey said. 'He's one of the best. As a skydiver, he won second place in international competition, and in two years when they hold it again, he'll probably come in first. I remember when he first started.'

'You've known Colin a long time then?'

'Longer than anyone except his

father, I guess. He never talks about him. But I understand his mother died when he was young. Once Colin let things slip and I figured out his father wanted him to go into the family business. When Colin wouldn't, the old man never forgave him. They never see each other now.'

Jennifer remembered her visit with Mr. Manning and Colin's reference to trying to see his father without success.

'He's a strange one, that Colin,' Whitey said. 'He lets me father him a little — give him some advice — but otherwise he's pretty much of a loner. Oh, he has girl friends from time to time,' he added, a twinkle coming into his eyes. 'Doesn't have one right now, though, unless the look I see him give you means anything.'

The memory of the day before made Jennifer's throat tighten. 'Not a thing,' she said, hoping for a nonchalant tone. 'I have no plans to be anyone's girlfriend right now, much less someone who doesn't know enough to stay inside a perfectly good airplane.'

Whitey laughed. 'Mind you,' he continued, 'I love that boy. When the right woman comes along, he'll make a good husband. He does everything the best he can.'

Jennifer grudgingly admitted to herself that Whitey undoubtedly knew Colin much better than she, but she wished he'd get off the subject of Colin's love life. None of it had anything to do with her. She was not that right woman Colin might be waiting for.

'And Colin is the strictest about the rules, too.'

'Who's strictest about rules?' Colin's deep voice interrupted the conversation, and Jennifer looked up.

'May I join you?' he asked. 'I'd like to hear more about this strict person.' His infectious grin brought a smile to Jennifer's lips in spite of herself.

'You know I'm talking about you,' Whitey said.

Colin signalled to the waitress and

ordered lunch. 'I don't think of my attitude as strict, just firm.'

'We were talking about the old days,' Whitey added. 'Since I don't jump anymore, I don't have many new stories to tell.'

'What old stories did you dredge up to amuse Jennifer?'

'I was going to tell her about the accident in Mendoza.'

Colin's smile disappeared immediately and a frown took its place. 'That's not a pleasant story. Why don't you forget it?'

But Jennifer's curiosity was piqued. She turned to Whitey. 'I'd like to know everything about skydiving. Please tell me.'

Whitey looked at Colin from the corners of his eyes, but slowly began the tale. 'It was a long time ago — ten years maybe — when Joe Paddroni killed himself — '

Colin sounded bitter. 'He didn't kill himself. You make it sound like suicide. It was an accident.'

'That's what *we* said,' Whitey argued, 'but you — '

In silence, the two men looked at each other. Jennifer felt they each remembered something different about the incident, and she suddenly had an overpowering desire to hear the complete story.

'What happened?'

Whitey continued slowly, his voice like a whisper. 'Danny Grover was the first to reach Joe, and he pulled off his parachute, got in the plane and jumped with it.'

Jennifer's voice rose in pitch. 'He jumped with the dead man's parachute?'

'Yep, bloody and everything. We would have stopped him, but we didn't realize what he planned to do.'

'Jennifer doesn't want to hear this,' Colin snapped.

'Danny was just a kid — '

Colin took over the story. 'There's no room for stupidity in this sport, no matter how young you are. I don't know what went through his mind, but he had just jumped himself and didn't have an emergency 'chute on.'

'Why would he do such a crazy thing?' Jennifer said.

'He thought he had to prove something. He knew Joe, and he thought he knew parachutes. He didn't think it had failed. He thought Joe hadn't pulled the ripcord.'

Jennifer spoke softly. 'So he put on the parachute and jumped with it and pulled the ripcord and — and it worked. He was right.' She visualized a youthful Danny, impetuous and over-confident, making his histrionic point.

'Or he wouldn't have lived to talk about it.' Colin added, 'I told you we shouldn't talk about this. It doesn't do any good.'

Whitey said, 'Danny told us he didn't want parachuting to get a bad name.' He paused. 'But he never jumped again.'

'Why not?' Jennifer asked.

'Because Colin kicked him out of the

school. Only time he ever did that.'

'If the foolish kid hadn't jumped with the parachute, everyone would have gone on thinking of it as an accident. But when it worked, it could only mean that Joe hadn't pulled the ripcord, that, for some reason, he wanted to die. Danny had done a terrible thing to his friend's memory. Darn near ruined the entire class. I couldn't let him stay.'

Whitey took up the story once more. 'Danny figured it out himself, of course, and I don't think he ever really wanted to jump after that anyway. Far as I know, he never took up the sport again.'

The uncomfortable silence that followed was mercifully broken by the waitress bringing Colin's lunch. Then Whitey changed the subject. 'As a matter of fact, we just arranged for Jennifer to take ground school.'

Too late, Jennifer flashed a warning look at the older man. He went blithely on, telling Colin all about their discussion and that she had just agreed to take the lessons. Her skin tingling, she wished she could stop him. Why did Colin have to know about her project? He might think her decision meant she had an interest in him.

'I didn't actually say I'd do it,' she corrected, 'just that I'd think about it.'

'Well, I've got to be going.' Whitey rose from the chair. 'You two can talk about it some more.' Pulling his billfold out of his back pocket, he walked toward the restaurant cashier.

Colin remained silent for a few moments, then, giving Jennifer a broad smile, he said, 'I'm glad Whitey left us alone. I wanted to talk to you. This past weekend meant a lot to me. I hope it meant something to you too.' He reached across the table and took her hand, where it rested near her coffee cup.

Slipping it free, she cleared her throat. He couldn't be saying he was falling for her — it wasn't possible. Their backgrounds were too dissimilar. Besides, there was that girl . . .

'I've been wanting to see you, too, to tell you that I think it's better if we don't . . . get involved with one another.'

His look changed. 'I don't understand.'

She couldn't bring herself to mention seeing the dark-haired girl hug him the day before — it would sound as if she were jealous. That was not the issue. He could have all the girlfriends he wanted. She just didn't want to be one of them.

'I'm sorry if you thought I was . . . attracted to you. Even if I were, it would be very unprofessional on my part to . . . ' She didn't finish the sentence.

As if a dozen different thoughts raced through his mind, his look changed again. 'Wait a minute, I think you misunderstood me. All I meant was that, in spite of a bad start, we seem to be getting along very well.' He shrugged, and continued, 'I meant that — ' He paused as if carefully choosing his words. ' — I'm sorry about what I did and what I said and I'm glad you accepted my apology so we can continue our tour as . . . good, er, buddies.'

She was grateful he seemed to have put no importance on the kisses in the cornfield, to say nothing of her response, and the less said about both the better.

He grinned at her, and again his look changed, as if this time he was plotting something entirely different from kisses in cornfields.

'So, you're going to take skydiving lessons,' he said suddenly.

'No, I'm not. Whitey tried to persuade me to do it, that is, just take the ground school lessons — I would never jump out of an airplane — but I didn't agree to it.'

'Why not? There's nothing about it that should frighten you. It might be just the thing to help you get over your fear of heights.'

'Why are you trying to get me to work overtime? I can hardly work time.'

Colin laughed with her. 'Didn't you

once tell me you were always interested in learning new things?'

'Yes, and I agree it makes sense for me to learn what preparations skydivers make, but — '

'Well, then — '

She remembered the many new things she'd done lately: putting on a sports promotion, roaring down a runway in an airplane, going to a skydiving exhibition, sleeping in a cornfield. She was no hothouse plant. She'd do it. Ever since she met Colin she kept doing things she wouldn't have believed. What was one more?

'Whitey tells me you don't have to jump for the first few lessons,' she said, 'only learn some basic things.'

'That's true,' Colin said. A smile turned up the corners of his mouth, as if realizing she had made her decision. 'And if you need any reassurance, I'll be right there to help.'

'Oh, please don't. You might just make me nervous.'

'There's nothing to be nervous

about. And, anyway, I have to be there. I'm the instructor.'

Of course he was. Hadn't he told her long ago that he taught skydiving? Why had she assumed some assistant would do it? Why couldn't he just stay in his office making major corporate decisions instead?

He picked up her luncheon check but she took it away from him along with his. 'Expense account,' she said, heading for the cashier. 'It's my turn for one-upmanship.'

11

Before Jennifer arrived at the field the next day, ready for her first lesson, she turned to the parachute manual Whitey had given her and read it three times. The book had called the parachute the safest piece of equipment ever invented, and took the next forty pages to tell all the things that could go wrong with it, and how to cope with them if they did.

If only she had never allowed Whitey to believe she would do it — if only Colin had not urged her to go through with it — she would never have shown up that day. But she couldn't solve problems by running away.

She had to continue the promotion, at least for the time being — until the opera house became a reality — and keep her word to take the first few lessons. After all, what could happen to her? No one had ever died taking ground school.

When Jennifer entered the office, four young men, all wearing jumpsuits, stood there talking and laughing. All were slender, two had short hair, one had shaggy locks, and one had a scraggly mustache. At the sight of Jennifer, the talking stopped, and they all took a long look at the only woman in their class, from her blonde hair tied in a neat pony tail, down to the obvious curves which could not be entirely hidden by the pale yellow jumpsuit she had rented. Determined to be just one of the guys, she strode forward and extended her hand to the man closest to her.

'Hi. Are you a new student too?'

They introduced themselves, and Jennifer asked about their reasons for wanting to learn sport parachuting. Their answers ranged from, ''Cause my Mom hates the idea,' to, 'Like, who wouldn't?'

'Have any of you read this manual?' She held up the little book she'd brought along with her. That started a lively discussion about what each of them had already learned, and then Colin entered the room and they sat down.

Colin went to the small classroom that had been created by putting some chairs in a semicircle facing a corner of the office, pulled out charts, diagrams and maps and began his lecture. Fortunately, he treated her no differently from the others, and, for the next half hour, Jennifer heard a repetition of what she'd read in the manual.

Colin's explanations made everything easier to understand, and it was a very informal session, interrupted, from time to time, with questions. Finally, Colin went to the long table against the wall and pulled it forward. On it was displayed an assortment of objects as well as a complete, packed parachute and one which was opened but contained no canopy. He explained the metal buckles, fittings and ripcords, and showed how they related to the parachute.

After that, he led them outdoors to where, one by one, they practiced stepping out of an airplane. They used a mock-up of an airplane strut and jump step — only a foot off the ground — and had to pretend they were exiting from the plane in mid-air, holding onto the strut and stepping onto the platform, then letting go and jumping into space. When all of them had done that several times to Colin's satisfaction, he then had them lie face down and practice the 'frog position,' stomachs down, backs arched, arms and legs extended but bent at elbows and knees. They practiced other falling positions, too.

Then they returned to the classroom for a lecture about possible malfunctions and emergency procedures. They learned what to do if a parachute inadvertently opened while still in the aircraft, or in the doorway, if the main chute didn't open, if both parachutes opened at once, or if the ripcord or static line dangled, how to jettison a malfunctioning chute, how to land in water, over power lines, in trees or on buildings.

Jennifer wondered again whatever possessed her to agree to take these classes, but she consoled herself by remembering that since she didn't actually intend to jump, she'd never be exposed to any of the risks Colin discussed so calmly.

Six o'clock arrived and Jennifer looked forward to returning to her apartment to a good dinner and an early bedtime. But then Colin announced that there would be a written test the next day on what they had learned.

At midnight she finally closed her weary eyes, and then she dreamed of parachutes, ripcords, static lines and altimeters, all jumbled together on top of her, weighing her down. When she awoke she found that during the night she had somehow wadded up blanket and sheets and piled them heavily on her stomach.

Like the four men, Jennifer passed

the written test. In fact, she had the highest grade, Colin informed her, grinning proudly. She smiled with genuine pleasure while accepting the congratulations of the others. She wanted to pass the test as much for her feeling of responsibility to her fellow students, as her desire to show Colin she could do it. She felt caught up in the spirit of it, just as she had always thrown herself wholeheartedly into everything. In a way she almost regretted that she would never actually do any skydiving and need to know any of these procedures. After all, she couldn't even go up in a plane.

She found her opinion of Colin changing as well, finding new aspects of his personality to admire. He taught brilliantly, bringing the class along step by step, making sure everyone thoroughly understood before going on to the next point. He would have made a fine teacher. In addition, he impressed her with his extensive knowledge of the sport, and his concern for safety.

But after the test, she learned he could be a rigid taskmaster as well. For their next assignment was to strap on parachutes and learn how to fall.

'Calf, thigh, buttocks, shoulder,' Colin thundered at them, and Jennifer muttered the words to herself as she waited in line. She wished then she had been more athletic in school, but gymnastics had never been her thing. Suddenly she had to throw herself on the ground as if landing after a jump. At her turn, she tried for the appropriate somersault type of landing, only to hear the men laugh uproariously at the attempt.

Colin smiled and said, 'Calf and thigh first, not buttocks. You surely don't want to bruise that part of your anatomy, now, do you?'

Jennifer saw nothing funny in it. Her backside did ache from the way she had fallen, but she wouldn't admit it for the world. Once more she got in line and tried again, that time managing to let her legs touch ground first, but still not exactly right.

'Once more,' Colin repeated, and they all moaned and repeated the process. 'And again,' he intoned, and Jennifer imagined her body, barely protected by the jumpsuit, must be covered with bruises.

The fact that some of the men also had to repeat the fall did nothing to improve Jennifer's reactions to Colin's sixth repetition of the phrase 'one more time,' and she almost agreed with one of her fellow students who muttered under his breath, 'If he says, 'one more time,' one more time, I'll strangle him with his own ripcord!'

She actually lost count of the number of times they repeated the maneuver, and just when she thought she could never force her aching body to do it again, he said, in accents reminiscent of Professor Higgins to Eliza Doolittle, 'Very good, I do believe you've finally got it.'

Jennifer managed a weak smile, thankful for the end of that, when Colin announced, 'All right, everybody, now we'll try the same thing from the four-foot platform.'

No dreams disturbed Jennifer that night — her exhausted body refused to allow them. She soaked for an hour in a hot bath, massaged every muscle she could reach and then collapsed into bed, thoroughly convinced she would never go back to that air field. He could threaten her with Chinese water torture and she wouldn't return.

However, the next day, either her stubbornness, her dedication to seeing everything through to its conclusion or just a desire to prove to Colin that she could take any punishment he could dish out, again brought her to the class, finding some consolation in the fact that her fellow students complained of aching muscles as much as she did.

Colin told them that the final day's classes would be 'easy,' then led them to another torture machine which contained harnesses. Each student strapped himself into one of the harnesses and was hoisted up so that he hung about two feet off the ground, then followed through one of the emergency procedures Colin would select. That gave them the feel of actually being in the air, dangling from a parachute, and having to make the maneuvers.

With harnesses for only four students at a time, Colin told the men to go first, assuring Jennifer that it would be easier for her once she'd seen the others perform.

But when her turn finally came, she decided it had not been altruism on his part at all, but a devilish desire to see her make a fool of herself all alone. She felt as if she dangled in the air for a lifetime, as she went through all the maneuvers, buckling and unbuckling, her hands sometimes refusing to cooperate, pulling on lines and dummy ripcords.

In the last maneuver she had to cut away a malfunctioning parachute and release her emergency. By that time every sore muscle sang its protests, and the men, who had already done the exercises, rested on the grass, laughing at her discomfort. She heard their teasing only faintly, trying to concentrate on the job, her feet leaden in their heavy boots.

'The parachute is streaming, Jennifer,' Colin called out. 'What do you do?'

'Cut it away?' she shouted back.

'Then do it,' he ordered.

She went through the correct procedure, and then had to pull the release rings to get rid of the main parachute. She yanked at them, but nothing happened. Cursing her weak hands, she yanked again, and this time one of them gave way, leaving her dangling by one strap, hearing a howl of laughter from the men on the ground.

Perspiration stood out on her face, her arms felt as if in some giant vise. Praying that it would work that time, she reached again for the release ring.

'Don't keep hanging there, old chum,' Colin shouted, 'Get hold of it and pull it harder.'

Jennifer knew Colin had been just as

stern with the men, but she began to resent him anyway. Using both hands on the ring, she pulled as hard as she could. It gave way and she fell in a heap on the ground, eyes closed, breathing heavily.

At a sound from above, her eyelids flew open and she saw Colin bending over her. She assumed he'd compliment her for her achievement. She heard him say in a soft whisper, 'Jennifer, that was lovely.' Then he added, 'but you're dead, you know. You didn't open your reserve.'

She clamped her eyes shut again and wished that when she next opened them she would be curled up in a cozy chair with a book in one hand and a box of Godiva chocolates in the other. And Colin nowhere in sight.

But after several minutes in the grass, she struggled to her feet, stalked back to the platform and climbed into the hated harness once more. In absolute silence — Jennifer wondered if the other students were offering up prayers for her — she went through all the procedures again, pulled the release rings as if they were the only things standing between her and death — and in a way they were — and, as she felt them give way, slammed her hand onto her chest for the emergency ripcord and yanked that too.

This time as she dropped into the soft green grass, she heard a cheer go up and then everyone clustered around her, hugging her and offering congratulations. After a moment, Colin had them all line up and he pinned funny little badges on their jumpsuits and kissed each man on both cheeks, like General DeGaulle rewarding his troops.

When he came to her, he smiled for a moment first, then planted a kiss on each cheek. She forgot her aches and pains when she looked into his eyes. He was no longer the cold-hearted instructor who had put her through torture, but her guide to achieving a personal triumph.

The men left the field, and they were

alone. She realized she didn't want the moment to end, felt as if something special had happened to her. She had already begun to establish a bond with Colin. Now she felt a stirring that filled her with both desire and confusion.

She remembered being in his arms, the touch of his lips on hers. Wait a minute! Why had she relived that moment, of all things?

The look on his face gave her the unnerving sensation that he could read her thoughts, that he knew she had undergone a change in her opinion of him during the three-day ordeal. No, she told herself adamantly, she would not change her mind about him. He might be a wonderful instructor, and she enjoyed the fleeting moment of having accomplished something, of having shown him she could do it, but she didn't want to be in his arms again. She was not falling in love with him. She wouldn't!

'Well,' she said, struggling to find some suitable words, 'that was — er

— a nice ceremony — an appropriate way to end the course.'

He took her elbow and began to lead her back toward the office. 'You know, I may keep that in from now on.'

She stopped walking and looked into his face. 'Are you telling me you never did that before?'

He grinned. 'It gave me a great excuse to kiss you again.'

'You — you — ' And then the thought of him kissing the men just so he could do the same to her seemed incredibly funny and she laughed. 'Serves you right.'

He draped an arm over her shoulder like a big brother, or a buddy, and they walked across the tarmac together. But she didn't feel the least bit like a buddy or his sister. The emotion growing inside her was much stronger than that.

* * *

Colin laughed with her, but deep inside he was disappointed that she had suddenly hidden the desire for him that had been so blatant in her face only moments before. Something had happened to her during those three days. It was more than becoming one of the skydivers, he was certain. He could almost feel her changing her opinion of him. But now she held it in check.

'You can jump on static line tomorrow,' he said.

'No thanks,' she answered, pulling off the harness of the emergency pack. 'I don't intend to jump at all. I never intended to take more than ground school lessons.'

'You haven't learned everything until you jump,' he insisted.

She was quite a woman, this Jenny Gray, brilliant in the written exams, brave and determined during the physical ordeal. Why wouldn't she go the last mile?

'There are some things I don't want to learn.'

His gaze roamed over her face and he tried to cover his frustration at her decision. 'That rather contradicts your earlier boast about being willing to learn new things, doesn't it? What is it you're afraid of . . . besides jumping?'

His accusation seemed to strike a chord with her, but she didn't answer. He lowered his voice, caressed her with his tone, remembering her body beneath his, pliant, surrendering, passionate. 'I can teach you that too, you know. If you let me.'

Still she didn't reply, and, with the other students already gone, Colin considered taking her in his arms again. Instead he forced his good sense to restrain his desire, and merely watched her turn and stride quickly away.

12

The long, narrow lake nestled among encircling trees, and Jennifer could see the tiny sparkling blue tip of it from her cabin. It looked cool and inviting. She knew when she left her air-conditioned room, and stepped out into the brilliant morning sunshine, it would be like walking into an oven turned up to 'Broil.'

She dressed in the coolest clothes she brought with her the day before, cotton shorts, sleeveless cotton blouse, and rope-soled sandals on her bare feet. She pinned her hair into a flat bun at the back of her head and added a straw hat with a brim. She added suntan lotion to her arms and legs, then slipped the bottle into her cotton string-tie bag before leaving the cabin.

She hadn't come to Millerton Lake with the others. She'd driven up the day before, put everything in readiness, finalized her plans for that exhibition, and arranged for the cabins for the twelve skydivers. Since the next day was July 4th, even Whitey Franklin had come along for the event, and everyone had decided to make it a long holiday weekend.

At first Jennifer had been glad to come earlier than the others. Otherwise Colin might have suggested her riding with him in his Thunderbird. And, although the thought of that wasn't exactly repulsive, she didn't want to set tongues wagging again. This was business, after all. Although she felt an unmistakable attraction to him in spite of his choice of occupation, she vowed to suppress those feelings. If she could survive ground school, she could survive a few more weeks of Colin Thomas.

But when the caravan of cars arrived the night before, she saw Colin climb out of his car with the same brunette she'd seen with him before. It had taken the rest of the night to convince herself her feelings had nothing to do with jealousy. True, she had become more affected by the man than she would ever have believed possible, but that kiss on the cheek at the airfield had been only a joke on his part. And, since she had already decided there was no romance with him in her future, she had no reason to get upset because he had a real girlfriend. She forced herself to think of nothing but getting her job done.

The heat had not kept people from attending the skydiving event and a huge crowd — used to summer temperatures in the 90's — turned out. A grandstand set up next to the airfield with a colorful red, white and blue canvas top provided shade, while on tall masts around the field, dozens of flags flapped in the summer breeze. A small band, which Jennifer had recruited from the local high school, played stirring marches.

She checked last-minute details with

Colin inside the hangar, maintaining a calm, businesslike attitude. But he reacted far differently to her.

'You've been running around all morning,' he said, catching her free hand. 'When are you going to relax and enjoy yourself?' His tone was sympathetic and his gaze searched her face as if for a sign she understood the meaning behind his words.

'Soon,' she answered, pulling her hand from his firm grip and putting a check mark next to an item on the list fastened to her clipboard. 'Your part in the program may be just beginning, but mine is far from over.'

'You've done a very good job, by the way.'

'Thanks.' She couldn't stop a smile that lifted her lips. She enjoyed the sincerity with which he spoke, appreciated his friendly attitude. If things were somehow different . . . But, of course, they couldn't be.

'I have you down for the water jump this afternoon.' She consulted her list. 'Is that right?'

'Yes. I did my quota of acrobatics for the year when I taught the class last week,' he joked. 'And how are *you* feeling these days? Have you recovered from our three-day entertainment?'

'Entertainment? Torture test would be more like it. And I'm sure my arms are two inches longer from hanging in the harness.'

'If they are, it's very becoming.' He moved closer to her. 'What about lunch?'

'There will be a break for lunch, of course. People can picnic on the lawn between the field and the lake. Although we have food vendors, most spectators have probably brought their own. I've arranged for some beach umbrellas to be set up, as well as the redwood tables and benches among the trees, so they can have a place to eat and a little shade from the sun.'

'Hey, slow down,' Colin said. 'I wasn't asking for your arrangements — I wanted to have lunch with you.'

That seemed an innocent enough

suggestion, but she wondered if he wanted to resume his attempt to seduce her. Didn't he take her at her word? Did he still think she might fall in love with him? And what about the girl he brought with him? Did he plan to make lunch a threesome? She sidestepped the question by saying, 'I thought you never eat before a jump.'

'I don't. But you do. Can't I watch?' He grinned.

She laughed in spite of herself. 'That doesn't sound like much fun.'

'Let me be the judge of that.'

'I'm sorry, but I must go now. It's starting time.' She fled before he could detect her too rapid heartbeat.

Like one of the paying customers, she sat in the grandstand to watch the events, forcing herself to concentrate on them instead of Colin. First came aerial acrobatics, with the jumpers performing dives, loops, turns and back loops in sequence. By watching the smoke flares attached to the jumpers' feet, she could keep track of the maneuvers in spite of their altitude. Then came formation jumps, four men making a diamond, or other shape, in the sky, and then three women came down together, holding a giant American flag.

Finally a 'star' — actually a circle — of skydivers holding hands took shape. Even after watching the jumpers get together to make their formations, excitement ran high as they leapt, one at a time, from the aircraft, and linked up with their hands. Although Jennifer had been told about 'stars' of over a hundred skydivers, she thrilled to it like a schoolgirl, and the audience applauded and whistled loudly when the twelve-pointed 'star' linked up perfectly. Then, seconds later, they broke from one another, and opened their parachutes.

Jennifer never did have lunch, because a bus filled with teenagers pulled onto the field, blocking the entrance, and it was almost time for the afternoon event before she had found the driver and, together with the security guards, convinced him to move the vehicle.

Colin stood on the field checking out the equipment on each of the men: first their two parachutes, then the flotation device for the water landing, and finally a waterproof bag for their instruments.

'You're late,' he accused when she approached, although his smile said he was happy to see her.

'I'm sorry. I had to settle a small problem, but the security guards have handled it now.'

'Speaking of guards,' he said, not looking up from his work, 'you did arrange to have people with life-saving experience in the boats, didn't you?' His forehead wrinkled into a frown.

'Of course.' She trusted that the young men she had hired were indeed as good as their reputations. All of the skydivers could swim, she'd been told, and all had made water jumps before, but it reassured her to know that an extra person would be available in each boat.

He handed a waterproof bag to one of the men and watched him attach it to his chest pack. 'Water will ruin an altimeter,' he explained to Jennifer, 'although not all of the men are taking one along on this jump.'

'Why not? Isn't it necessary?'

'Not really. It's true that there's less depth perception over water than over land, and jumpers have been known to be injured thinking they were only a few feet above the water when actually they were forty or fifty feet above, but the boats will give them a point of reference today. Besides, they're not supposed to let go of the harness until their feet touch the water.'

'My schedule says only six of them going up at a time. Is that right?'

'We need a jumper in each boat. Then we'll take turns.' He smiled and winked. 'Want to come along and jump with us?'

'Not on your life. But I might watch you from one of the rowboats.'

He turned and went to the plane, calling over his shoulder, 'Some day you'll do it.'

Jennifer ran the entire distance from field to lake and arrived just in time to see the six small rowboats, two men in each, push off from the sandy beach to get into position to pick up the skydivers after they landed in the water. She shouted to Mike Drummond, who waded next to one of the boats, 'Mike, may I go with you?'

'Sure, come aboard.'

She pulled off her shoes and hat, leaving them in the sand, and waded into the cool clear water, letting it splash on her legs. She scrambled aboard, and the other young man, looking like a teenager, wearing only swim trunks and a deep tan, helped her to the middle seat. Water swishing softly against the sides of the boat, they rowed to the middle of the lake and, with the other five boats, formed a large circle.

Then Dave, the lifeguard, put on swim fins and slipped a face mask onto his head, where it rested in his tightly curled sun-bleached hair. Prepared, they watched the jumpers leave the aircraft one at a time, free fall for several seconds, then open their parachutes and maneuver them toward the target in the center, a rubber life raft with a bulls-eye painted on cloth.

One by one they landed near the target, and as soon as they did, the boat which had been assigned to that particular jumper, went out and picked him up. Jennifer's boat picked up the last jumper of that group, and she watched in fascination as they gathered in the parachute and then dragged it ashore. Mike left to take his turn in the air, and the man they had brought back to shore peeled off his jumpsuit, shoes and helmet, revealing his swim trunks underneath, and got into the rowboat, ready to be the experienced skydiver required by regulation.

Again they were to pick up the last jumper, and Jennifer realized it would be Colin. He usually came last in any of the exhibitions, being jumpmaster, but he was also the best, so it always looked as if he'd been saved for that position.

Watching him leave the aircraft, Jennifer felt a surge of pride, then stopped herself. Hey, since when was she responsible for his superior performance?

His jumpsuit whiter than chalk in the sky, he spread his arms and legs for his stable free fall. She stared up, not heeding the ache in her neck from constant sky-watching, and thrilled as his chute opened and the colorful canopy snapped him upward for a few feet before it began its descent to the water.

She thought she could almost see him begin to unfasten the harness buckles that held him in the parachute and get ready to release it so that he wouldn't be dragged down with the fabric when it became waterlogged and heavy.

As usual, he landed right on target, his feet touching lightly onto the bulls-eye on the raft. Then he let go of the handles on the chute and it drifted above him momentarily and finally settled on the surface of the water.

As Dave rowed toward it, Jennifer watched Colin slip off the raft into the water, reaching for the chute before it had time to sink. The sight of him, immersed to his chin, brought a rush of emotion. She stood up in the boat, leaning forward to help him pull in the soggy parachute.

'Sit down,' Dave said to her. 'We can handle it.'

She sat down obediently, but never took her eyes from Colin's head as he tugged at his equipment in the water. Then he slipped beneath the surface. And stayed. And stayed. What could he be doing down there all that time? Didn't he need air?

Suddenly a terrible thought struck her. What if he was tangled in the chute and couldn't get loose? She jumped overboard and dove under the enormous parachute. Colin hung head down in the water, untangling the lines of the chute which had somehow become caught in the cable which held the life raft to its anchor. He wasn't in danger at all.

She felt incredibly stupid: underwater, hair streaming, blouse swirling around her waist. Who did she think she was, the patron saint of skydivers?

Her splash had alerted Colin and he looked toward her, eyes questioning. She helped him untangle one of the lines, but quickly ran out of breath. But before she could turn and swim away, the parachute imprisoned her. The descending canopy settled over her and she felt herself sucked underneath. She fought its clinging folds, tried to get down and around it, but was trapped. Panic rose like bile in her throat. She couldn't hold her breath much longer.

A hand grabbed her arm and pulled her forcefully in the other direction. She felt herself dragged down. She would drown. But, just as suddenly, the water became lighter in color and she discovered Colin had pulled her away from the chute and they surfaced.

She broke water with a sputter and

gulped hungrily of the fresh air. Colin's head bobbed up next to her, and they both tread water. He grinned at her. 'You thought I was in trouble, didn't you? You like to manage everything.'

She wouldn't admit for the world that she was trying to save his life and tried to think of a clever retort. 'I only wanted to help you free the lines. Anyway,' she added, 'it was getting awfully hot in the boat. I thought a little swim — '

He laughed loudly. 'You were only in over your head again, this time literally as well as figuratively.' The rowboat had come near, and, boosting her up, he shoved her into the waiting arms of the two young men on board.

'Gee, Miss Gray,' Dave said, helping her sit on the narrow bench, 'I'm awfully sorry. I should have been watching. I didn't realize I tipped the boat so far that you fell overboard. But you shouldn't have been standing, you know.'

It was nothing she wanted to explain

to the young man. Let them think it had been an accident. In any event, Dave no longer looked at her anyway. He had resumed pulling the parachute to the side of the boat.

Colin clambered aboard and grabbed an oar, helping to row the craft back to the beach. As soon as it scraped the sand, he helped Jennifer out, found her sandals on the beach and handed them to her. 'But next time you decide to go for a swim, don't you think you should be wearing a bathing suit?' She could hear him laughing all the time she squished back to her cabin.

While she peeled off her wet clothes, toweled dry and pulled a comb through her hair, she tried to analyze her behavior. Somehow Colin had become the object of her every waking thought. Why had she suddenly felt protective toward him? She hadn't fooled him for a moment with that, 'I just dropped in to help' routine. What dumb thing would she do next?

Then she remembered the brunette

he had brought with him. How did she fit into all this? For that matter, where had she been hiding all afternoon? It was a mystery Jennifer suddenly wanted to solve, even though it might not be prudent.

13

Jennifer had no time to ponder the problem of the girl Colin had brought with him — she was still in charge of the promotion and there was more work to be done. Dressing in cotton slacks and a fresh sleeveless blouse, she left the cabin, settled accounts with all the people she'd hired, saw that the skydivers' gear was locked up for the night, checked on the picnic supper and the wood for beach fires, and talked to the fireworks handlers who had been arranged jointly by Jennifer and the local Kiwanis Club. Finally, just as her chores ended, darkness settled over the field. The fireworks would begin any moment. She headed for the beach to join the others.

Several driftwood fires dotted the beach and Jennifer sauntered toward them. Recognizing Whitey and Mike, she joined them, roasting hot dogs and passing around huge paper containers of potato salad, bean salad and coleslaw. The buns were soft and warm and the relish tasty, and though normally she didn't care for hot dogs, she had to admit they were delicious that night.

Other fires, marking other picnics, glowed on the beach, where many of the townspeople had stayed to watch the fireworks from that vantage point, but after the brilliant display ended and the sky deepened from blue to black, they drifted back to their homes, leaving only the skydivers who would not be going home for another day.

Mike Drummond had brought his guitar and, as he played folk songs, Jennifer joined in singing the familiar words. Then someone shouted, 'Do you know what?' and answered his own question with, 'It's too darned hot!'

'Let's go swimming,' someone else suggested, and soon they rushed to their cabins to change into swim suits and plunge into the water. Jennifer went to her own cabin and changed to her cranberry-red bikini.

The water refreshed her, even if it did seem almost as warm as the surrounding air, and there was something mystical about swimming in the dark. The others laughed and shouted, playing games in the water, and some just sat on the sandy bottom with water up to their chins, telling jokes or the usual parachute stories.

Although she hadn't seen them that evening, Jennifer assumed Colin and his girlfriend were together somewhere, and she felt superfluous. She swam out to the raft anchored not far away, and pulling herself up, sat down on its slippery wooden surface. Alone, nothing more to do at last, she could think about Colin objectively. They were friends, right? Nothing more, no matter that every time she saw him her brain seemed to turn into goulash. And as for him — well, he had started out acting like a man trying to make time. But, after she had rebuffed him that night in the cornfield, he had apparently decided she was off limits and had turned to someone else. So why was she so upset about it? Wasn't that what she wanted?

But the memory of those kisses — even the memory of the ones on her cheeks after completing ground school — continued to haunt her. And seeing him with another woman was making her miserable.

There was just one way to handle that. Get over it. She'd made her bed, now she must lie in it. She re-tied the ribbon around her hair and took a few deep breaths before getting ready to dive into the water and return to shore.

Suddenly she felt a touch on her foot, and let out a startled gasp. The water broke around her and then Colin's head bobbed to the surface.

'You,' she said. 'I didn't see you swim up.'

'I came the last twenty yards underwater.' Tiny drops glistened on his chiseled features and mat of black hair, and dripped from his exposed muscular shoulders.

He pulled himself effortlessly onto the raft and lowered himself next to her. 'You look marvelous every time I see you, but I had no idea you had posed for the cover of the swimsuit issue of *Sports Illustrated*.'

'Just a moment — ' Fighting down the tendency of his eyes to hypnotize her, she tried to think of a snappy comeback, but none came. Instead her body had begun to shiver in spite of the summer warmth.

'You must have been reading my mind, too,' he continued. 'I've been trying all night to think of a way to get you alone.'

Jennifer turned away, not wanting to look into his face. This was just too confusing, like having two men to deal with instead of one. The first Colin was conceited, chauvinistic and had a girlfriend. The second was intelligent, well-mannered and seemed to crave her company. Would the real Colin Thomas please stand up?

She faced him again, found her voice at last. 'You seem to be forgetting something. What about the young lady you brought here last night? Where does 'getting me alone' leave her?' As soon as the words left her lips, she regretted them. Why had she brought up that subject? He was a free agent and she had no right to question his choice of companion, especially when she had made it clear to him that she wasn't interested in a romance.

'Young lady?' Colin repeated, his look thoughtful. 'Oh, you mean Billie.'

Jennifer tried to smooth things over. 'Is that her name? You didn't introduce us.'

'That's because she's never where she's supposed to be,' he said irritably. 'Besides, everyone knows Billie — I've been dragging her around to jumps since she was six — ask Whitey, ask anyone. She's my little cousin.'

His cousin. She tried to hide her sigh of relief, but Colin noticed.

A broad smile spread across his face. 'Were you jealous?'

'Of course not.' The new information changed nothing. Comforting, but hardly a reason to let down her guard again. Still, it wouldn't hurt to be polite. 'You may scoff about my feeling that we're very different kinds of people, but — '

'But you intend to fight it out on that line if it takes all summer,' he finished.

She had to laugh at his turning a quotation to his advantage. 'I'm only here to do a job, remember?'

'You don't have to do it every minute. Live a little.' He stood up and pulled her to her feet, and suddenly his wet body pressed against her and he kissed her soundly. Her lips instinctively parted under his, and her body tried to melt into him. His naked torso against the bare skin between the two halves of her suit could have been 200 degrees instead of wet and cool for what it did to her.

'Hi, you two.' A voice at their feet

made them break apart like guilty teenagers. Billie climbed onto the raft.

'Jennifer, this is my cousin Billie Shoemaker, a little genius at showing up in the wrong place at the wrong time.'

'Hello, Billie. I'm glad to meet you. I've heard so much about you.' Suddenly, Jennifer saw an opportunity to put some distance between herself and Colin and took it. 'Why don't we swim back to the beach together?'

She took a last look at Colin. The moon cast a silver light on his features, emphasizing the rugged planes of his face, making him look like an ancient Greek statue. Electrifying. She wanted nothing more at that moment than to succumb to that hard body, to be in his arms again. But she still had no intention of falling in love with him. True, his kiss had made her heart pound and her head dizzy, but he was not her type, never would be. The entire experience was like an exotic Hollywood production, a scenario played out in strange new places. It would all end when the tour ended and reality returned. Until then she had to hang onto her sanity. Billie's arrival, along with the cool water of the lake, might shock her to her senses.

'What if I don't want you to go?' Colin teased, reaching for her hand.

'You have to be a fish, not a skydiver, to keep up with me tonight.' She dropped into the water, exhaled deeply, and slipped deeper. Then she kicked furiously, heading for the beach. Two could play at that underwater swimming game.

She finally broke the surface yards away from the raft, and turned her head to look back. Billie dove in, taking after her, but Colin stayed on the raft.

* * *

He watched them stroking easily over the gentle ripples of the water. Perhaps it was just as well Billie had come along when she did. Otherwise he'd have made love to Jennifer right there on the slippery, rocking surface of the raft. Or would he? She still responded to his kisses, but, even without his cousin's sudden appearance, he suspected Jennifer possessed enough strength to keep him at bay at least a while longer. What he needed to know was how this would end and, more importantly, how he wanted it to end.

14

Jennifer spent most of the next two days at the lake with Colin before everyone drove home. That had not been her intention, but it worked out that way. On Sunday Mike and Sandy organized a day of activities for the skydiving club and, although she protested she wasn't a member, they insisted she'd be a spoilsport if she didn't participate.

Actually, she enjoyed it, swimming, boating, walking in the woods, and — especially — talking to the wives of the other skydivers and getting to know Billie. She decided the girl was an enigma, eighteen going on thirty-five, and definitely a free spirit. In spite of the obvious comparison to Colin, whose carefree life-style she seemed bent on emulating, there was a firm core of independence in the girl, and Jennifer concluded no one would ever take advantage of Billie, no matter what.

And then, after lunch, having dozed under the shade of a tree, she awoke to see Colin sitting nearby.

'You're even beautiful when you sleep,' he announced when she discovered his presence.

'I'm told I snore.'

'Not a bit. It's the sound of a butterfly inside a flower, or a cool mountain stream brushing against a fallen tree, or — '

'My, we're very poetic today, aren't we?'

'You shouldn't patronize me when I'm being lyrical. Those moments are all too rare, as you yourself should know.'

What Jennifer knew, all too clearly, was that Colin had many sides to his personality, most of them unexpected. Part of her wanted to find out more about him, while another part resisted, afraid to get too involved. She straightened up from her position in the grass and leaned back against the trunk of the tree.

Her inquisitive side won out. 'Did you ever write any poetry?'

'Didn't everyone? It was more or less a required school subject. What about you?'

'Yes, a little, in fourth grade, I think.' She smoothed her hair, adjusting the ribbon that held her pony tail.

'When you were in fourth grade, did you wear your hair in a pony tail with a ribbon in it?'

'Two pony tails,' Jennifer corrected, 'one on each side. And the ribbons always came undone.' She got up and began to stroll back to the lodge.

'Your ribbons came undone? No way.' He fell in behind her on the narrow path. 'Other children's ribbons, perhaps, but not yours. I can't imagine you as anything less than 'Miss Perfect,' right to the tips of your pony tails.'

'I was a normal child,' she insisted, and picked up a loose twig from the ground and threw it playfully at him. 'It was only later that I became perfect.'

His hearty laugh sounded through the clear, country air. 'When did you begin to read to the blind?'

How had he learned about that? Did she tell him? She couldn't remember.

'During high school. I went out for the school play and missed getting the leading role. To mollify my hurt feelings, the coach suggested I try the debating team, because I had a pleasant voice and good articulation.'

'A very pleasant voice,' Colin agreed. 'But not good enough for the school play?'

'Thank you. My voice may have been good, but my timing was completely off. I should have tried out for the play two years earlier, before Ginger Ferris got there.'

'What did Ginger Ferris have that you didn't?'

'Red hair and something going with the acting coach.' After she said it, Jennifer walked faster, hoping to put more distance between Colin and herself. Having brought up the subject of romantic liaisons, she worried he'd continue, say something about the obvious sexual attraction between them. She felt her body wilt at the remembrance of his embrace on the raft the night before, and a warm liquid sensation made her knees suddenly weak. Something physical, primitive even, made her want him to touch her again. It had nothing to do with love, she told herself.

'You're also very persuasive,' Colin said, 'which I'm sure has come in very handy in your present work.'

She smiled. 'You're right. I spend a lot of time convincing people to do what I want them to.' She paused. 'Even when it's for their own good.' She laughed, knowing a little self-righteousness was one of her faults.

'Like trying to convince me I shouldn't be a skydiver?' he asked.

She slowed her pace. 'Did I ever tell you that?'

'Not in so many words. But you certainly give off the strong impression that anything unconventional meets with your disapproval.'

'Just because I don't fly — '

He interrupted her. 'It's more than that and you know it.' When she didn't answer, he changed the subject. 'When did you start making cassette tapes for blind students?'

She swung around to look at him. 'How did you find out about that?'

'I have spies everywhere.'

She shrugged. 'In high school, and then in college I read textbooks to a blind student.'

'Did you fall in love with him?'

Jennifer felt her heart beat stronger. Why did Colin mention love? That remark, together with the news of his obvious attempts to learn more about her, made her feel like the object of an F.B.I. investigation. Or something more intimate. 'No,' she answered, 'not that it matters.'

'I'm glad you saved yourself for me.'

He skipped ahead of her in the path, turned around and walked backward.

She looked squarely at him, ready to remind him that she had no intention of getting involved with someone whose best friend might knock at her door one day with bad news. But she didn't. She determined to keep the conversation at that light level.

'Since you're not blind — and can walk backwards without tripping — I don't see how I can help *you*.'

'Oh, I'll think of something.' He grinned.

'What did *you* do in high school?'

'All the usual things big healthy boys do: football in the fall, basketball in winter, baseball in the spring.'

'And in the summers?'

'Worked in one of my father's companies. Every year a different one, some of them quite far away. He wanted me to learn about them all.'

'It sounds like a very good idea.'

'I suppose so. That way, when I took over as president — ' He cleared his throat with a loud 'ahem' and emphasized the word ' — I wouldn't be resented because of being the boss's son.'

'How perceptive of your father.'

'A brilliant titan of industry, no doubt about it,' Colin answered, but his voice had taken on a hard edge.

'Your father — ' Jennifer began.

Colin interrupted her. 'I don't want to talk about my father. Let's change the subject. I'd rather talk about you. Your life is far more interesting than mine.'

'Me?' Jennifer laughed. 'Miss Conventional?'

'But the more I learn about you, the more I find you're not so stodgy after all.'

'If that was a compliment, thank you. But you don't think *your* life was interesting, every summer in a different company, learning new things?'

'I resented it. First of all, you have to remember I went to a private school. I wasn't at home with my parents during the school term. So, when summer came, I wanted to be there, and he wouldn't let me.'

'Did you tell your father how you felt about it?'

Colin turned about and faced the direction in which they walked, pausing for a long time. 'No, I couldn't tell him. He never seemed to understand me. Besides, he was so much older.'

'Could you tell your mother and ask her?'

'My mother died when I was nineteen. I was away at college and I didn't even know about her illness until too late. I received a telephone call in the middle of the night, and by the time I arrived home, she was gone. I never got to say good-bye to her.' His last words barely audible, his pace accelerated so that he took huge strides down the path, and Jennifer almost had to run to keep up with him.

'Colin, please slow down. Colin, I'm so sorry.'

He stopped and turned to her, his features under control again.

She stared into his eyes. 'You blame him, don't you?' she asked with sudden realization. 'You blame your father. That's why you didn't want to go into the family business.'

'I'm an adult now. I don't blame him any more.'

'I think you still do.' Another thought struck her. 'And I think you took up skydiving because it was a dangerous sport.'

'You think I wanted to kill myself and then he'd be sorry for the way he treated me, is that it?'

'You tell me.'

'Perhaps I did, just at first, but I soon realized three things. I liked the sport, it wasn't all that dangerous, and I loved my father.'

'So you've tried to reconcile with him.'

'Not lately,' he admitted, 'but when I used to go there regularly and try to talk to him, he always ignored me.' He paused. 'I guess I said some pretty horrible things to him when I was angry about my mother.'

'But you were young, and hurt. You can't be held responsible for saying things you later wish you hadn't. We all do that.'

'Not George Thomas Manning.'

'He was hurting too, you know. He loved your mother and was just as unhappy and upset as you were.'

'I know all that, believe me I do. That's why I wanted to talk to him, but he refuses to see me, and, frankly, I haven't even tried in several years.'

'I think you should try again. When I spoke to him the other day, he seemed — '

'There you go again,' he accused, but with a light tone, 'trying to arrange people's lives for them.'

'Okay. It's none of my business.'

They had reached the row of cabins by then and he suggested a swim. Later, as they had dinner with the others, he told stories about his first airplane ride and his first parachute jump, and Jennifer decided he seemed like the old Colin again. She liked that Colin and determined not to feel anything stronger for him.

15

Early the next morning, before the sun was fully up, Jennifer heard a light tap on her door and Colin's voice.

'Wake up, sleepy head,' he whispered. 'I have a surprise for you.'

She tiptoed to the door and opened it a crack. 'What surprise? Can't it wait until daylight?'

'What?' he asked, mocking, 'and let the whole world know what we're up to?'

A momentary doubt crept into her mind, but she quickly dismissed it. Colin seemed bent on wooing her with charm, humor and surprises, not heavy-handed pressure. Not that it would do him any good, of course, but she could at least be polite and join in the fun that always seemed to be going on around him.

'Can I get dressed first?' she asked then.

‘Yes, wear pants instead of a skirt and take a sweater.’

She closed the door and pulled on her clothes hurriedly. A sweater in this scorchingly hot valley? Of course, it was still early, but —

By the time she had finished dressing, combed her hair, put on a little make-up, and joined Colin on the path between the rows of cabins, the eastern sky had taken on a pale glow.

‘Well, here I am. Where’s the surprise?’

For answer, he simply took her hand and led her to where his Thunderbird was parked. They got in and drove away from the campgrounds. Jennifer kept asking about the surprise, but he only grinned and said nothing, so she finally turned on his car radio and found a music station.

After about twenty minutes, they were out of the trees and into what appeared to be miles and miles of vineyards. Soon he turned off the highway onto a dirt road.

'Colin,' she entreated again, 'please tell me where we're going. What is this surprise?'

He pulled into a large dirt parking lot, which seemed decidedly out of place among grapevines, and turned off the ignition. 'Remember, you don't have to do this if you don't want to.'

'Do what? Colin Thomas, you are the most exasperating — '

'Fly.'

'Fly? Colin, you know I'm afraid of flying. Anyway, this isn't exactly Los Angeles International. I don't see a single airplane.'

'They're not here yet. Besides, it won't be an airplane.'

'A helicopter is just as scary as an airplane, in my opinion. Anyway, didn't you tell me once that they're dangerous, that you can't glide them in like you can a plane if they lose power, and they just drop like a rock?'

'It's not a helicopter.' He paused, watching her face. 'Remember a couple of weeks ago you mentioned my having a hot air balloon packed in the trunk of my car?'

She didn't remember, but what he was now proposing did flash through her mind with lightning speed. 'You want me to go up in a balloon?'

'To overcome your fear of flying. Step three. When you mentioned a hot air balloon the night my car broke down, I sort of filed the idea in the back of my mind. It seemed like a good way to introduce you to getting off the ground.'

She felt her heartbeat quicken. Could she do that? Wouldn't it be even scarier than going up in something with wings and an engine?

When she didn't answer, he continued. 'Pretty soon some vans and trailers will pull into this parking lot and they'll have balloons with them. They'll inflate them right over there — ' He pointed out the windshield to an area in the midst of the nearest vineyard. ' — and some people will get in them and go for a ride. I hoped we could go too. But you don't have to,' he added again. 'You can just watch if you'd rather.'

'I don't mind watching,' she said. 'I've seen balloons from a distance. They're so beautiful.'

True to Colin's prediction, a yellow van appeared on the road and then pulled in next to them. Three men and three women got out, and one man went around to the back of the van and pulled out a large chest. Another retrieved two large thermos jugs, while two of the young women picked up pink cardboard boxes.

By then two more vehicles had arrived, an old station wagon and a pickup truck towing an open wooden-sided trailer that was filled with a large mound covered with a black tarpaulin. Colin unfastened his seat belt and came around to Jennifer's side of the car to open the door. They strolled over to the others and Colin introduced her.

'Have some coffee and sweet rolls,' one of the women, whose name was Margaret, invited.

The tailgate of the station wagon lay open and someone had spread a small tablecloth over it, then placed the open bakery boxes on it along with the thermos jugs which turned out to contain coffee and tea. A carton of cream appeared as well as a box of sugar cubes, some white plastic spoons, tall stacks of styrofoam cups and a package of paper napkins.

While she gratefully drank some hot coffee, Jennifer listened to Colin and the others talk about ballooning. Another van arrived and so did another truck and trailer. She noticed that the men who drove the trucks gulped their coffee quickly and then got to work unloading their cargo. Balloons.

They were carried to the cleared-off area, released from their dark coverings, and spread out on the ground. Strange machines and fans were brought up and soon everyone was involved in getting ready to fly. Air was heated with propane and then forced into the bags by the fans, and little by little the flat, colorful mounds of cloth began to take shape and billow up from the earth.

Jennifer walked around one of them, admiring its brilliant rainbow mosaic, amazed at its size.

'What do you think?' Colin stood at her side, sipping his coffee.

'I don't know. They're so beautiful, aren't they? But they only have those little baskets.'

'Not so little,' he said. 'They can hold seven people. So we won't be alone.'

'Let me think about it some more.' She was grateful he put no pressure on her, and was amazed to find that — so far at least — the thought of possibly getting into one of those baskets and going up into the sky didn't turn her legs to jelly. She walked away from him, back to the station wagon where, suddenly realizing this might be her only breakfast, she took a sweet roll and chatted amiably with the others.

From that distance she watched the rest of the preparations. Soon two enormous balloons stood in the field, brown baskets below, long ropes hanging down from all four sides. One was striped with every color of the rainbow, and the other was lemon yellow with huge red flowers and green leaves.

Colin returned and, taking her hand, led her back to the balloons. 'Come and see up close.'

She held onto the side of the basket and looked up into the balloon where a propane heater blasted hot air into the top. A young man, Ziggy by name, was already inside, and in one hand he held a rope that connected to the heater, while the other held a cell phone.

'He keeps in touch with the chase car on the ground,' Colin explained, 'so when the balloon comes down, the van will be there to bring us back.' He paused. How about climbing in for a moment to see what it feels like?'

'You won't take off yet?' she asked Ziggy, and he laughed and said he needed a full load of passengers.

She climbed over the side with

Colin's help and then he climbed over too. So far so good. She felt no need to clutch onto him, although the basket rim was only slightly higher than her waist. But she was still on the ground, so of course she wasn't afraid.

She looked up into the huge canopy again, and thought how comforting it looked up there, even if it was made only of nylon and thread.

The basket came up off the ground and then bumped down again. 'We need more people here,' Ziggy shouted. Then three of the women and another man joined them, climbing in and grinning. Still Jennifer didn't feel afraid. Was it because there were so many of them, so close? Or was it just the nearness of Colin?

His arm went around her waist and he leaned close to her ear. 'If you don't want to go up, you're going to have to say so right now and we'll get out. They want to start.'

Where was the panic? Why was she so calm? 'I guess I'm okay,' she said. 'But stay close to me.' She put both hands on the edge of the basket and felt Colin's arm tighten.

'You're fantastic.' Then he said loudly, 'Tally Ho!'

Everyone laughed, someone said, 'Hey, this isn't a fox hunt,' and the balloon left the ground again.

This time it kept ascending, and Jennifer watched the ground drop away beneath the basket. As it did, her heart began a trip-hammer dance in her chest and she thought she'd just made the biggest mistake of her life, that any moment she would scream or sit down on the floor of the basket and cry like a baby. The knuckles of her hands whitened in her fierce grip on the basket edge, and her rate of breathing increased.

Then Colin put one finger beneath her chin and turned her face to his. 'You're going to be okay. You're going to make it. Breathe slowly, deeply. Relax.'

For several minutes the balloon went

up and Jennifer refused to look anywhere but in Colin's eyes. There was something about him, a quality that made her feel safe with him, at peace. She sensed that nothing terrible could ever happen to her when he was near. She felt her tension give way.

Then, abruptly, the noise of the blower stopped and a serene silence took over. She turned and looked out at the sky and fields. It was incredible. A picture postcard. Slowly, almost lazily, they drifted in the early morning air currents, as silent as a butterfly.

The other balloon had risen by then and she watched it move gracefully away. The occupants of the two baskets waved to one another. Then the blower was turned on again, and they went up higher to get over the crest of a hill dotted with deep emerald trees.

'Look,' she said to Colin, releasing one hand from the edge of the basket and pointing, 'there's a pond down there and a swan swimming in it.'

'So there is.' He grinned at her,

looking proud and happy, seemingly aware of her triumph over fear.

Jennifer liked it best when the blower was turned off and they floated quietly across the vineyards and fields. When they came to some taller trees, she felt as if she could reach out and pull off a leaf. Amazing.

They flew for about thirty minutes altogether and then the pilot pointed out the chase car and told them where they would be landing. He pulled on lines, releasing air from the top of the balloon, and they descended into a field. Three men from the chase car grabbed the ropes when they came near and pulled the basket close to the ground. Taking turns, some got out of the basket and others got in for their ride. Jennifer and Colin climbed out and got into the van for their trip back to the parking lot. They didn't speak to one another until after they had said good-bye to the remaining balloonists, got into the Thunderbird and drove back toward the highway.

'You're smiling like the cat that ate the canary,' Colin said.

'I have a right. I still can't believe I did that. I flew!'

Colin began to sing. 'Those magnificent men in their flying machines — '

Jennifer joined in, 'They go uppity-up-up. They go down-de-de-down-down.'

16

The sheets a wrinkled mass on her bed, and the flowered spread thrown carelessly to the floor, Jennifer woke from a restless night. Even her calmer moments of sleep contained dreams of billowing parachutes, or soaring balloons, with Colin's handsome face superimposed on the images, a smile playing about the corners of his lips. It didn't really surprise her that her thoughts centered on him. After a long weekend of almost constant companionship, she could think of no one else.

She gave up trying to sleep, in spite of the early hour, pushed the sheets aside, and ran the water for a long soak in the tub. She sprinkled a large amount of bubble-bath crystals into the foam of water cascading from the faucet and drank in the scent for a moment before plunging into the slippery warm water. The tenseness of her muscles gradually gave way to the gentle lapping of the bath water, but her mind continued in as much turmoil as ever.

How could she possibly handle her feelings for Colin? She had to face facts. She was definitely infatuated with him, all but powerless to resist his advances. Was it his good looks, his mastery of a difficult and exciting sport, or something in each of them which had a magnetic pull to the other? She didn't know.

She did know that her entire adulthood had been one of acting in exactly the opposite way, making plans and then following through on them. She had always insisted she wouldn't ad-lib her way through life as her mother had. She would know precisely what lay ahead. Cold and calculating, she admitted, lathering her body slowly, but it didn't have to be. She didn't necessarily intend to choose a husband just because he held a high-status position, but rather she believed one could as easily fall in love with that kind as any other. She'd never believed in only one right man for every woman. There were always choices, and a sensible woman waited until the stirrings of love and desire coincided with the man who had the other qualities she considered important.

And then Colin Thomas had come along and thrown all her theories off the nearest cliff. She enjoyed his company, but that was because the entire promotional tour was like one giant holiday. The real world would intrude soon enough and she would be back to making sensible decisions. Meanwhile, she would not be swept off her feet by the wrong man, no matter how much her body yearned for his.

She tried to remember the first kiss she ever received back in high school, her first date, the first boy who meant anything to her — hoping to put Colin into that category — someone who had struck her fancy once, but whom she easily forgot when someone better came along. But Colin would not be forgotten. He haunted her dreams, becoming an integral part of her daily life. At least while this promotion lasted. After that, as much as she might want Colin to give up skydiving for something more conventional — and though she knew she had a penchant for trying to get others to see things her way — she hadn't, and never would, try to change him. She would simply let him go out of her life, which was inevitable in any case, when the tour ended.

In fact, perhaps the promotion needn't last much longer. It had been weeks since she'd spoken to Mr. Manning about the opera benefit. Perhaps he had good news for her and hadn't been able to reach her due to the skydiving events. She'd telephone him later.

After dressing and eating breakfast, she drove to her office and plunged into the mail that had accumulated during the long weekend. Her boss appeared at her doorway.

'I haven't seen you for a week,' Peter said, without entering. 'How's the project coming?'

She smiled at him, then returned her gaze to her desk. 'This promotion is much more complicated than I ever imagined. You can't believe the amount of paperwork involved.'

Peter seemed on the verge of coming into her office but then changed his mind, fingering the doorknob as if nervous about something. 'How about lunch?' he asked. 'There are a few things I'd like to talk to you about.'

Jennifer didn't hesitate, realizing his request was a business command and not a social engagement. They went to La Maison, a French restaurant where the food was excellent. Jennifer, who loved the delicate flavors of French cooking more than any other, enjoyed the meal. As they finished with coffee and *creme caramel* for dessert, Peter finally brought the conversation around to business.

'I should be angry with you,' he began.

'Why?'

'Because you went over my head. That just isn't done, you know.' His friendly tone belied his somber words.

'I don't understand.'

'You went to see George Thomas Manning, to try to get his support for the opera promotion.'

She felt her face grow warm. She had forgotten about that, hadn't realized Mr. Manning might contact her boss. What a fool she'd been not to discuss it with Peter in advance. Now what? Would he retract his promise to let her do the opera promotion?

'I'm sorry,' she said, pushing her half-eaten dessert away and looking down at the napkin in her lap. 'I shouldn't have done that. I'm afraid I acted without thinking.'

'Impulsive gestures often get people into trouble,' he said, 'although I can understand why you did it.'

'You can?'

'I haven't known you very long, but I think I've learned quite a bit about your character already. You plunge into whatever you're doing with such enthusiasm and energy — trying always to do the best — you sometimes get carried away.'

'Yes, I guess I do.' She tried to do her best, yes, but, get carried away, act impulsively? Not usually. However, lately — But it was better to agree with the boss at all times.

'I knew you wanted the opera benefit more than anything else. I should have anticipated, I suppose, that after I made that promise to you, you might try something like this, just to get out of the skydiving events.'

'Oh, it wasn't that,' Jennifer protested, although she knew that certainly had been her original purpose, and then, flustered at having told a lie, she squirmed, twisting the napkin around her fingers. 'I mean, it wasn't just that.

Yes, I did want to get out of the sports promotion because, as I told you — ' She looked up, hoping her expression looked sincere, ' — I didn't feel qualified, and I had wanted the other for so very long.'

'But you're doing a splendid job, just as I knew you would.'

'Thank you, but at the time — well — ' She stopped. She couldn't go much further down that line of explanation. She couldn't tell Peter what had transpired between her and Colin. She had never been a person who discussed her love life with others, and she wouldn't start now. She really did want to do the opera promotion. She had to make Peter agree without seeming to have manipulated anyone.

'I've tried to do a good job of the skydiving tour,' she finished lamely.

'I know you have,' Peter acknowledged, 'and believe me, I'm not angry about what you did. In a way I approve your obvious enthusiasm and the fact that you showed resourcefulness in visiting Manning to organize things. After I got over my initial embarrassment when he telephoned and I had to admit I had no idea you'd been to see him, I came to the realization that you're a person who believes first and foremost in getting things done.'

That part of his assessment of her was true, anyway.

Peter paused before continuing. 'Well, I didn't mean to scold you. I hope you don't think that.'

'No, I understand.'

'I'm very pleased with your work. In fact, I've decided that, since you obviously have made progress in getting the opera funding, I'm going to release you from the skydiving tour now.'

The offer startled her. She hadn't expected him to let her out of the commitment at that point. 'Oh, really, Peter, that isn't necessary.'

'What? You just said you didn't feel qualified and that you wanted to do the other — '

'I am. I mean, I do. I mean — ' Good

grief, she sounded like an idiot cleverly disguised as a responsible human being. 'I know this probably sounds strange, but I've actually come to enjoy the promotion. I guess you were right after all — '

'What do you mean?'

'What I mean is, why don't I finish the tour — since we're so close to the end anyway — and *then* I can work on the opera promotion. Another three weeks won't make that much difference, I'm sure.'

'That's very generous of you, but you don't have to, you know. I can put Dan Smith on it — '

'No, no, I'd really like to finish what I started. But thanks for giving me the option, anyway. That's very nice of you.' She tried to hide her sigh of relief.

'Well, if you're sure — '

'I'm sure.' She looked at her watch. 'As a matter of fact, tomorrow I have to drive to Fairmount about the exhibition there and probably won't get back until the next day. So I have a lot of things to do. I really ought to get started.'

Peter signalled the waiter and lay his credit card on the tray. 'Then I guess we'd better get back to the office.'

The truth was that Jennifer needed to get away and think over what she'd just done. Why hadn't she pounced on the chance to be rid of the skydiving promotion? Wasn't that what she wanted? True, she did like to finish whatever she started, but deep in her heart she knew the reason she balked at giving up the tour was spelled 'Colin.' She wanted to go on seeing him.

Yes, he was not right for her. Yes, she must not encourage him. Yes, she was in danger of falling in love with the wrong man. But she shoved those thoughts aside. As she told Peter, three more weeks wouldn't make that much difference. Surely she could remain professional and detached for that short a time.

She went back to her office and put all of her concentration into planning Colin's next two promotional jumps. The first exhibit would be held in nearby Frazier Park, a night jump into a circle of lights.

She drove there alone on Friday night, found Colin wearing a silver jumpsuit. He seemed to have a variety of them, blue, white, orange. She guessed he had chosen the silver one that time because it would sparkle in the lights.

Whitey joined Colin and Jennifer in the pavilion in the center of the park. 'Reminds me of the old days,' he said, rubbing his chin thoughtfully. 'I used to love making night jumps.'

'Well, come on,' Colin urged. 'Come with me.'

'No, no,' he protested. 'I'm too old to jump anymore. Anyway, you're teasing me. It's your show. You're the star.'

Colin tilted his head back and emitted a full-throated laugh that carried across the park. 'I'm not a star,' he denied. 'I'm just a guinea pig. They push me around, here and there, doing stunts so someone can make some money for charity.'

'But people look up to you, like you're some sort of god,' Whitey said. 'I know all about it. I used to love that feeling myself. Gosh, doesn't everyone like attention?'

Colin's gaze met Jennifer's and she knew he was thinking about the reason he had gone into skydiving. It definitely wasn't to be the center of attention. He could probably have been a lot more famous — like his father — if he had stayed at home.

An official from the park interrupted them, and for the next hour Jennifer took care of final details, double-checked the program sequence, and talked to the men in charge of the lights.

The cocktail party held before the jump raised funds for the charity, and guests, dressed in attractive party clothes, mingled in the balmy evening air and strolled on the grass of the park, leaving their empty champagne glasses everywhere except in the receptacles provided.

Work done, Jennifer found Colin on the airstrip and said the usual, 'Good luck.' Then, impulsively, she took off the pink silk scarf she'd been wearing and tied it around his neck.

'What's that for?'

'Your silver jumpsuit looks like a suit of armor. Didn't ladies back in Camelot give scarves to the knights before they went off to joust or something?'

'It was supposed to bring them luck in the battle. Also' and he paused, ' — it meant he was performing for the love of the lady of the scarf.'

Oh. She reached out to take it back, but his hand caught hers in mid-air. He didn't speak, only looked into her eyes. She was about to protest that he needn't bother performing for *her* love, when Whitey came up and told him the sky was dark enough and it was time to go.

Colin's plane took off and the spectators found their vantage points to watch the jump. The lights of the little pavilion flickered out, leaving only the circle of headlights made by strategically parked cars. Jennifer watched with Billie, who had insisted on seeing her cousin's night jump.

Colin, a mere dot in the sky, left the plane and began his descent. The battery-powered lights, about the size of small flashlights, fastened to his wrists and ankles, lighted him as he free fell to earth, and she spotted him against the darkened heavens. Then his parachute opened and a spotlight flooded on, illuminating the interior, like a giant cradle of light. Brighter and brighter he became, his silver jumpsuit shimmering like sparkling water, and then he landed, perfectly, in the center of the circle of the car beams.

Billie joined the crowd of people who rushed forward, but Jennifer watched from a distance as they crowded around him, the young girls touching his jumpsuit, shoving autograph books at him. He caught Jennifer's look once and gave her a lopsided grin and shrugged, as if to say this was really an unpleasant part of the job, but somebody had to do it.

She waved at him, then busied herself seeing that the lights of the pavilion went on again, so people could gather back at the bar for a final glass of champagne and more conversation. She thanked the officials and everyone who had helped, then watched as couples returned to their cars. However, since Colin had brought Billie in his car, she left as she had come, alone. She felt like Tom Hanks in *Cast Away* but didn't even have a friendly volleyball to talk to.

17

A week later the blue Thunderbird stopped in front of Jennifer's office and Colin stepped out and came around to hold the door open for her. She held her plum-colored cotton skirt neatly as she got in, conscious of his scrutinizing every inch of her legs. The same dual feelings returned — she enjoyed his admiration and hated herself for it.

But if she had any fears that she wouldn't be up to the task of keeping those feelings in check, they proved unnecessary. The first words he spoke to her while he steered the car skillfully away from the curb and into the light traffic, were, 'Whitey is coming with us. We're picking him up at his apartment.'

So she wouldn't be alone with Colin on the long drive after all. She almost sighed aloud, but it left her wondering if that was due to regret or relief. She wanted to ask for her scarf back, to relieve his mind of any false notions that she was interested in a romance with him, but, on the other hand, she hesitated to bring up the subject of their relationship. If they didn't talk about it, perhaps it would go away.

Within a few minutes they had picked up Whitey, and the three headed out of town. Seated between the men, Colin's right arm pressed against her shoulder, she enjoyed the drive, although she barely spoke at all for the first hour. Colin and Whitey kept up a steady stream of conversation, commenting on flying, jumping, parachutes and old times. She really loved hearing about the escapades they had had in the past, the practical jokes some of their friends had played on others.

Finally, Colin apologized for their having talked over her head for many miles and changed the subject. Then they drove into the Los Padres National Forest, beyond which lay their destination.

The road wound slowly up the mountains through thousands of tall crowded trees. Gradually their conversation slowed until it stopped altogether, and gradually too, it occurred to Jennifer that something was not quite right. An acrid odor hung in the air, and she realized what she could see of the sky above was no longer blue, but gray.

Just as she decided to ask him about it, Colin snapped on the car radio and said, 'I think there's a fire somewhere.'

After fiddling with the dial for some seconds, he finally found a news station, and amidst crackling of static, they heard the announcement that, because of the extremely dry weather, a fire had started in the Los Padres forest.

Almost immediately they came to a sign on the highway which read, 'Fire Danger High,' and a little farther, at a fork in the road, a uniformed forest ranger could be seen setting up a road block. Colin stopped in front of him.

'Take this road to the left,' the man commanded.

'Where's the fire?' Colin asked.

'About five miles from here. Too close for safety. You'll have to get down this way,' and again he waved them toward the other road.

'Which way is the ranger station?' Colin asked then. 'Are there any smoke jumpers there? I'm a parachutist.'

The ranger paused a moment before replying. 'If you want to volunteer, come with me. I'm going near there now.'

Colin pulled on the emergency brake, then stepped out and went around to the trunk.

Jennifer's heart pounded. 'What are you doing?' She knew: he intended to leave them and go off with the ranger.

'I'm going to volunteer,' he responded, lifting out parachutes and suitcases.

'What does that mean?'

'Smoke jumping,' Whitey answered for Colin. 'We've all done it. You jump into the area and help fight the fire.'

'But you're not firemen,' Jennifer protested, 'you're skydivers. I don't understand.'

Whitey explained patiently. 'Lots of sport parachutists also become smoke jumpers. They jump into a forest fire area where other ways might be impossible. They can help contain the fire or even put it out.'

By then Colin had retrieved the gear he wanted and hauled it to the ranger's car at the side of the road. Jennifer jumped out and ran to him. 'But isn't that dangerous? You could be killed.'

Colin put down his bundles and turned to her, but before he could speak, she changed the subject. She couldn't let him think his personal safety meant so much to her. 'What about the promotion?'

He had been about to say something, but he paused, his lips in a thin hard line. 'Postpone it,' he said tersely, turning away from her.

'Postpone it? Do you realize how much work went into this? Do you understand the plans that will have to be changed, the schedules, the people who will be inconvenienced?'

He stared down at her with an intense look. 'Yes,' he said in a low voice, 'I know that, but people live in and near this forest. Their lives are in danger. That's all I care about right now. If I can help stop the fire from spreading, that's my first priority, not the promotion. I'm sorry, but that's the way it is.'

'But the contract — '

'Don't you understand?' he continued. 'This is more important. I'm an experienced smoke jumper. I have to go.'

Jennifer couldn't be angry because everything he said was true, but frustration and fear threatened to overwhelm her. The smell of smoke had become heavier in just the past few minutes, and the sky seemed darker. She even felt warmer, as if the fire already touched her bare arms.

She didn't want to think about Colin jumping into it with his parachute. Would the chute catch fire? Would the smoke overcome him? If skydiving itself was dangerous, then what about smoke jumping? It sounded like a *kamikaze* mission. Her heart almost stopped beating.

'They didn't call you to come,' she pleaded with him, tears suddenly stinging her eyes. 'You don't have to do this.'

Colin finished stowing his belongings in the ranger's car and turned to her with a slight smile. 'You're afraid for me,' he said, making it more a statement than a question. 'You do care, don't you?' and before she could reply, he swept her into his arms and gave her a hard, passionate kiss that left her breathless.

Then he turned her about by her shoulders and pointed her to the Thunderbird. 'Take my car down,' he said. 'I'll probably be here for two or three days.'

'But how, what . . . ?' She stumbled toward the car, tears blurring her eyes.

'Don't worry,' he answered. 'I'll get someone to bring me back when we're through. Whitey,' he added, 'take care of her.' Then he jumped into the other vehicle and it sped off.

Jennifer stood helplessly in the road, watching the departing car, frustrated over Colin's decision to leave her, angry with herself for selfishly wanting him to stay, worried for his safety. It wasn't fair.

She wanted to scream aloud, to throw herself down on the ground and kick her heels, but the moment passed quickly. Even as a child, she'd never had temper tantrums. Now she was a grown woman and a practical one at that. She knew she had to accept the situation and try to muddle through.

Whitey, who had been silent during the last few minutes, spoke quietly to her. 'Do you want me to drive?'

'No,' she said firmly, 'I'll do it.' She climbed in behind the wheel, glad to have something physical to do.

Grim-faced, biting her lower lip, she sped off on the left-hand road and they descended the mountain. After a quarter of an hour, the strain gradually began to leave her, and Whitey, apparently sensing her relaxation, began to talk.

'Don't worry,' he said. 'It's not all that dangerous.' In a slow, soft voice he related to her how smoke jumpers worked: jumped into the area with protective covering, carrying axes and shovels, and blocked the progress of the fire.

Jennifer listened, her mind only half on his words, the other part beginning to wonder how she would postpone the promotion, rearrange so many plans. His abandoning her so suddenly, leaving her to rearrange the promotion, made her anxious, but on the other hand, how could she be angry with someone who risked his life for other people? It was one thing to jump in front of spectators, win trophies and enjoy the tribute of the crowd. She already knew he didn't think much of that. But quite another to behave heroically when no one else would even see or hear of it. Her worries for his safety mingled with pride for his decision.

A question from Whitey interrupted her thoughts. 'I'm sorry,' she said, 'my mind wandered. What did you ask?'

'I said, you don't think I'm too old, do you?'

'Too old for what?'

'To get back into skydiving.'

She looked at him, puzzled. 'I don't know, Whitey. I guess if you were just starting for the first time, people might think so, but you've done it before. You're experienced.'

'That's right,' he said, forcefully. 'It won't take me long to get ready. I'm not worried about forgetting anything, but I'd do a little practicing on the jump stands just to get the feel of it. I might even jump with Colin at Fairmount, especially now that it's been delayed. How long will it be delayed?'

'I don't know. That's up to Colin now.' Sudden despair filled her tone. 'He may *never* come back.'

'Of course he will.' He told her about his own experiences as a smoke jumper, about the time he had to dig a trench for himself, lie in it and cover it with earth when he was trapped in the path of an approaching fire. 'And, see,' he ended, 'I'm still alive.'

'Oh, Whitey, you are a good friend. Thank you for telling me. I can't help being a little afraid though.'

'Oh, he'll come back okay,' Whitey assured her. 'He's very resourceful. Besides he has you to come back to.'

Jennifer whirled her head around to him and saw the smug, 'I-know-your-secret' look on his face.

'Whitey, you don't understand,' she admonished. 'We're not — I mean, I'm not — that kiss you saw didn't mean anything.'

'Sure.'

'Really. I'm not in love with Colin and he's not in love with me.' There, she'd settled that matter once and for all. Then why didn't saying it make her feel better?

'I can't speak for you, but I've known Colin a long time. I'd say he cares for you.'

'Well, I don't care for him,' she insisted. 'He's arrogant and opinionated and chauvinistic.' None of that was true and she knew it, but the words sounded irrefutable. 'And he jumps out of airplanes for a living.'

'Oh, well,' Whitey said, a shrug in his voice, 'if you want someone perfect — '

Perfect. Of course, that was it. She'd been denying her feelings for Colin because she convinced herself he wasn't perfect. And not only Colin. All her life she'd judged men and found them lacking. They were too pushy, too laid back, too indecisive. When they reacted to her good looks, she dubbed them shallow and sensuous, only interested in one thing. No wonder she never formed a close relationship with a man: she immediately found fault with all of them. Unless they looked as she thought they should look, spoke with the proper language and inflection, believed in exactly the same things she did, she wrote them off. No human being could possibly live up to the unrealistic standards she set.

Her mother hadn't waited for a perfect man, but married the one she loved. It had been a good marriage, Jennifer knew. The size of his paycheck never kept her mother from loving her father, from showing it when he returned every evening. Their marriage had few material things, but it certainly had happiness.

She felt the heat rise to her cheeks and she realized how wrong she'd been. What had her mother said about pride? Why, the word didn't begin to describe the cold, heartless reality of it. She had put herself on a pedestal and believed a man who did something she couldn't approve was beneath her.

The gnawing frustration that had marked the past few weeks suddenly dissipated, replaced by a surge of strength, of peace, of acceptance. She didn't have to fight it any longer. She could admit it. She loved Colin!

Sobered by her sudden realization, she tried to sort out what it meant. Okay, she could accept what he did for a living, but what about Colin? Would he accept her, faults and all? He had never said he loved her although he often acted as if he cared a great deal. But kisses — even passionate ones — were not necessarily indicative of a desire on his part to continue their relationship after the tour was over. Men often wanted what was close at hand, but could forget about it just as easily when out of sight. There was even a song about it, with a line that went something like, 'I love the girl I'm near.'

She would have to be wary of allowing her feelings to show, just in case they were not reciprocated. It was bad enough to have to admit it to herself, but, if she told him and he thought there was no future for them, possibly even laughed at the notion, she would risk being humiliated.

18

A sullen, overcast sky hung over the airfield when, two weeks later, the postponed promotional jump was about to take place. Jennifer had spent the time handling the always necessary paperwork connected with skydiving events, undoing everything that had been done for the earlier exhibition and making different arrangements. That required countless telephone calls, trying to soothe the irritated heads of charitable groups, airport managers, skydiving club officials and — it seemed — everyone listed in the Stafford phone book.

Since she was an organized person, work usually never depressed her. Which was why she found it hard to understand her feelings. Sure, it was frustrating to have to rearrange everything she'd done before, but her depressed state of mind stemmed from another source entirely: the fact that this was the next-to-last exhibition. The tour would soon be over and she might never see Colin again. Once, that was what she wanted, now the concept haunted her.

But how could she manage to tell him? Liberated or not, she couldn't call him up and say she'd changed her mind and was now ready to take him as he was. She had to wait until she saw him again, then let him know of her change of heart. Would he see it in her eyes?

And how did Colin think about her? He had made the first overtures regarding their relationship. He said he cared for her, kissed her fervently, held her in his arms on several occasions. In spite of the many times she'd rejected him, did he still feel the same way? Now that she knew her own true feelings, he suddenly seemed aloof and distant.

She hadn't seen him since the fire,

although they'd talked on the telephone. He spoke briefly, almost curtly, then apologized, saying he had something on his mind. They'd handled their business and hung up, leaving her to wonder if he thought her shallow for her comments about the tour, or if his passionate kiss meant more than he could discuss. Just what was the something on his mind?

Colin's long strides covered the strip of grass on the air field, and she saw a tense, worried look on his face. She felt her heart constrict. He wasn't going to postpone the jump again, was he?

'Colin, is something wrong?'

A frown creased his forehead and he said almost brusquely, 'Why did you encourage Whitey to take up skydiving again?'

'I didn't encourage him,' she answered, surprised by the question.

'He said you told him to go ahead.'

Jennifer felt attacked and backed up instinctively. She tried to remember her first conversation with Whitey on the subject. 'I said that, since he'd been a skydiver once, he probably could get back into it without too much difficulty. I didn't encourage him. He asked my opinion and that's all I said. Colin, what's the matter?'

He ignored her question, continuing his argument. 'He's too old for the sport. Good grief, I'm thinking of giving it up soon myself, and I'm thirty years younger.'

Giving it up? Was he serious? If so, it explained his coolness toward her since returning from the forest fire. Making such an important decision must be what troubled him. But why? A thousand questions sprang to her mind.

'You can't do this kind of thing forever,' Colin said, as if trying to convince himself. 'Your reflexes have to be sharp. It takes tremendous physical stamina.'

'I thought you told me lots of older people participate in the sport.' She paused. 'But, even so, why should what I say have any influence on Whitey? I had the distinct impression he had already made up his mind to do it before he asked me, and even if I had said I thought he shouldn't return to skydiving, he wouldn't have listened.'

'He wants you to look up to him, to admire him — '

'Of course I admire him. We've become friends. But I know next to nothing about skydiving. Why should he care what I think?'

'Ever since you came around, he's been acting differently: dressing up, asking the guys to watch their language when you're around — '

'That doesn't mean anything but courtesy — '

' — He follows you around like an adoring puppy — '

'He's tried to help me with the exhibitions, that's all. I'm grateful.' She didn't know whether to be happy or upset. She didn't like being the object of Colin's anger, but did his apparent jealousy mean he loved her?

'He's been practicing every day for

the last two weeks, and he bought some new equipment and is all set to jump today.' Colin flung the words at her as if she intended to push the man out of the plane with her own two hands.

'I don't understand why you're so worried about him,' she argued. 'You're the jumpmaster here. If you don't want him to jump, tell him so. He has to obey you, doesn't he? Aren't you in charge?'

'He does everything right.' Colin's irritation worsened. 'There's really no way I can stop him, no technical way. And he's my friend, too. I can't hurt his pride by suggesting he's not up to it, or that he's not smart enough to realize it.'

Her heart went out to Colin. What concern for his friend. It endeared him to her, even if his fears were probably unfounded.

'Besides,' Colin went on, 'I have no right to interfere in his life. I resented my father doing it to me.'

'If he's been a superior skydiver,' she said, 'why are you worried? He told me he made thousands of jumps.'

'Years ago, yes. This is now.'

'Has he passed a recent physical?'

'Yes, damn it. I told you there's no technical reason I can stop him.' He thrust one hand through his thick black hair and heaved a sigh. 'You're right,' he said in a low voice. 'I shouldn't have said what I did to you. Whitey's a grown-up and is entitled to make his own decisions. Who wants to live like a hermit?'

In spite of his words, she knew he was still worried. She touched his arm, wanting to soothe him. In the distance she heard the revving of the airplane engines that indicated time was short. 'It will be all right,' she said, 'you'll see. We're all on edge. I think it's the weather that's making us jumpy. We'll feel better when the sun comes out.'

'You're probably right. I'd better get back to the hangar.'

When he left, Jennifer realized Colin's worry had now been transferred to her. She really did like Whitey and wanted him safe. But surely he would be. He had never seemed happier than during the last few days, anticipating his first jump after so many years. And he had experience, after all. But no matter how she tried to chase the gloom, it refused to obey. And weather had nothing to do with it.

The sun still had not appeared when the meet began. The spectators filled the bleachers, the band played, the master of ceremonies told funny jokes, yet Jennifer remained as downcast as the clouds. She sat on the sidelines, watching, and the skydivers jumped from the plane, did their maneuvers in mid-air, opened their chutes and landed.

Because of the low-hanging clouds, the planes didn't go as high as usual and the jumpers were clearly visible, but they had much less time to do aerobatics and stunts before pulling their ripcords. Although she had seen it a dozen times before, the thrill remained. If anything, it was stronger that day, since it might be the last time she would ever watch skydivers in person.

Then Whitey jumped. Her heart seemed to leap into her throat and stay there. She watched him do a front loop and then a back loop. A little ragged, perhaps, but acceptable. He had not gone up there, after all, to win a prize that day — he had told Jennifer that he just wanted to compete.

One more back loop and then he would pull the ripcord.

But something was wrong. He looked out of control. Instead of arms outstretched in stable position, he held one hand pressed against his chest. Jennifer thought he was going to pull the ripcord, yet her few lessons told her he was doing it wrong. Down, down he came, like an untidy bundle discarded from space.

Jennifer jumped to her feet and ran to the edge of the field. Forgetting the crowd, she screamed, 'Pull the ripcord!' The band, which had been doing a low drum roll, waiting to burst into a fanfare when the chute opened, stopped playing. A hum of excited voices came from the stands. Other people stood up, staring into the sky.

Just when she decided to close her eyes — that she couldn't bear to watch any more — the pack on Whitey's chest erupted and a small parachute blossomed into life. He had pulled the emergency chute instead of the main one.

But he was too close to the ground. No, not the ground, the hangar. He had made no effort to place himself over the field, and time had run out. His body made two oscillations and, then, swinging widely, he slammed into the hangar and fell the remaining fifteen feet to the ground.

The field exploded into action, everyone running forward at once. Shouting into his microphone, the master of ceremonies tried vainly to keep the crowd in its seats, but the people ignored him. Jennifer, already halfway to the scene, reached Whitey's side almost at once, but Colin, who had not yet gone up, blocked her way and grabbed her roughly by the shoulders.

'You don't want to see him,' he growled. 'Stay back! Get the people back in their seats. I'll handle this.'

Suddenly remembering her responsibilities, she turned around and staggered back toward the visitors, urging them to go back, yelling for the police and security guards.

Chaos reigned on the field for almost half an hour before order was gradually restored. Whitey was taken into the hangar, the doors closed, and the spectators, deprived of anything to watch, gradually returned to the bleachers and the exhibition continued. The M.C. announced shortly that Whitey Franklin was alive and being taken to the hospital, and then, moments afterward, an ambulance did arrive, remained briefly and departed.

Jennifer sat in a daze through the rest of the afternoon, torn between wanting to go to the hospital to be with Whitey and her attention to duty. But the day had been spoiled for everyone, and after watching a few more jumps, the crowd dispersed. Nothing that a skydiver did after that could equal the heart-stopping excitement of Whitey's fall.

Jennifer didn't see Colin again. He never made his jump, never appeared after the accident. Lethargically, she wandered about the field, watching the cleanup crews, talking in low tones to other parachutists, pilots, their friends and relatives. When everyone else had gone, she remained behind, unable to summon the energy to walk to her car. Although she could logically leave the field and go to the hospital, she felt reluctant, wanting to postpone the moment when she might hear bad news.

She wandered into the hangar again and this time noticed the parachute on the floor; Whitey's, the one he had pulled at the last moment. It looked like a silky bed sheet thrown in a heap. She sat down on it, grabbing its folds with shaking fingers. She almost imagined she could keep him alive by holding onto the chute itself, and she found herself saying prayers that he would be all right.

After a long time, she lay down on the nylon fabric, turning on her side and bringing her knees up, hugging them with her arms, as if rolling herself up tightly would keep out the terrible memory of what had happened to her friend.

Incredibly, she slept. The traumatic event had taken its toll, and the next thing she knew, there were sounds in the distance, a car driving up and stopping nearby, its engine cut abruptly. Then silence for a moment until the door of the hangar slid open, screeching on its tracks. Her eyes sprang open and she was surprised to see darkness had taken over the huge room. She must have slept for hours.

She turned and twisted upward at the same time, coming to a sitting position, and tried to peer into the gloom to identify the person who made heavy footsteps on the floor. When he stood over her, she recognized Colin.

'I see we're both drawn to the scene of the crime.' He spoke bitterly.

'How is Whitey?' she asked. She would have risen, but Colin sank down beside her, rested his arms on his upraised knees and lowered his head between them wearily.

'He's alive,' he mumbled.

'What happened? Why didn't he open his main chute? Is he badly hurt?'

Colin raised his head and turned to her. 'He had a heart attack in mid-air.'

'A heart attack!' Then she remembered. 'But the physical? You said he had just had a physical.'

'Yes, that's what I asked the doctors too. In fact, I probably shouted it at them. My God, how could they let this happen to Whitey? It's a miracle he's still alive. Somehow he realized he didn't have time for the main chute and pulled the reserve instead. He's in critical condition but they won't say anything more until morning.'

Jennifer touched his arm. 'He'll be all right. I know he will.'

'Why did this happen?' Colin demanded. 'Why him?'

'We don't know why some things happen. There's no one to blame.'

'I do, though,' he answered, and his voice took on a hard edge, rising in pitch. 'I blame the doctors. I blame Whitey for trying to go back into skydiving at his age. Most of all I blame myself. I should never have let him go.'

'You couldn't have known this would happen.'

'I knew, somehow I knew. I told you this afternoon, didn't I? I had a dread of his jumping, but I couldn't find any legal reason to stop him. Just my intuition. But I should have listened to that.' He pounded his fist into his knee with such force that Jennifer flinched.

She knew she mustn't let him go on blaming himself. 'It's not your fault,' she repeated. 'Accidents can happen to anyone. You did the right thing, according to what you knew.' She remembered something else. 'Why, only a week ago, Whitey told me you were the best jumpmaster he'd ever seen, that your jumpers always abide by the rules and you have the best safety record in the entire state.'

'It wasn't enough,' Colin railed, his voice cracking. He pressed his palms into his closed eyes, as if trying to blot out the image of Whitey's fall. Silence surrounded them for long moments, while Colin remained too choked to speak, and Jennifer searched for something helpful to say.

'In my heart I know I'm responsible. What am I doing here, holding the lives of all these people in my hands?'

'That's not true,' Jennifer insisted. 'You didn't force anyone to become a skydiver, certainly not Whitey. He made jumps when you were a child. People know the risks before they start, and you, of all people, have probably saved dozens of lives by proper teaching and insisting on safety measures.'

'Don't try to exonerate me,' he said in a desolate voice. 'I should never have gone into this in the first place. I tried to prove something, and now look what I've done. I've almost killed the one friend who meant anything to me.'

Hardly pausing, he went on, and Jennifer knew she mustn't interrupt him, that he must pour out his anger and frustration, talking to himself more than to her, and perhaps it would end with his coming to terms with this tragedy and with whatever other demons were bothering him, holding him prisoner.

'My father was successful. He wanted me to take over his business, but I wouldn't do it. We had a terrible quarrel and I turned away from him and his business and never went back. I was going to show him!' He paused at last. 'Whitey has been like a second father to me — I guess that's why I love him so — I've been substituting him for the real father I turned my back on.'

'It's not too late,' she said softly.

'Whitey is still alive, and so is your father.'

'I said such terrible things to him. I accused him of murdering my mother.'

Jennifer's breath caught in her throat. 'Murdering — '

'I don't mean really murdering. I mean I blamed him for her death. I wasn't there, and I thought if he hadn't sent me away to school, there would have been something I could do — '

'At nineteen? Colin, you were just upset. It was perfectly natural to feel that way. But I'm sure your father did everything possible for your mother. He loved her.'

'I know that now, but at the time — He was so much older than I. We were never very close. I couldn't speak to him like other boys spoke to their fathers.'

'He probably regrets that as much as you do — '

'There was only my mother and when she died I blamed him. I'd been expected to go into the business so I refused, just to hurt him. But of course that was foolish. I went back to apologize, but he wouldn't see me. Then Whitey came to work for me, and he's been my best friend. Now I'm about to lose him, too.'

Jennifer put her arms around his shoulders. He turned his head toward her and then, with an explosion of pent-up emotion, whirled his body around, caught her in both his arms and kissed her fiercely.

His body pressing, he pushed her back on the parachute's nylon fabric and almost at once his hard, muscular frame was over hers with such force she felt momentarily helpless to protest. His lips left hers and he moaned her name in her ear. His mouth rained kisses on her cheeks, her forehead, her neck. She whispered his name, stroked his face, trying to calm him, to make the moment tender as well as passionate. She loved him and wanted him with every fibre of her being. She would surrender to him at last, tell him of her love.

For two weeks she'd visualized their making love with sweet tenderness, but somehow it didn't matter that her dreams were replaced by a totally different reality. She was through making plans, trying to force life to fit her preconceived mold. If he wanted her now, here in a deserted airplane hangar, then that was how it would be.

All that mattered now was that she knew that she loved him and her need was as great as his. 'Colin, I want to tell you something . . . '

As if her words brought him back from a trance, he broke away from her. His body tensed as if he were a marionette on a string, and, his face close to hers, she saw his eyes fill with pain, that perfect mouth retreat into a thin line.

Quickly, he moved away from her, got to his feet.

'Colin,' she said, leaning toward him in the dark. 'What's the matter?'

'It's not you.' His voice rasped. 'It's

my fault. I never seem to learn, do I?'

'Learn what? Colin, I don't understand,' she pleaded. 'I want you too. I'm not pulling away from you. I love you.'

He had already reached the doors, slid them back noisily on their tracks and fled from the hangar.

'Colin, don't leave me,' she called to his retreating back, but she knew he wasn't listening, even if he could hear her words. In seconds she heard his car start and drive off. With a cry of anguish, she threw herself face down on the parachute, feeling its hard folds under her body. Great sobs wracked her, and she ground her fists into the nylon, inviting it to burn her raw.

What had she done? Now that she loved him, he didn't want her. She had lost him forever. And her cries echoed through the hollow building.

Much later, she walked out of the hangar toward her car, her legs feeling wooden, as if they didn't belong to her. As if someone else were opening her car door, turning the key in the ignition, driving away from the air field for the last time. As if the last ten weeks were only a dream or nightmare from which she'd awaken.

19

Colin arrived at the Lake Tahoe cabin almost unaware of the trip. Not once, he admitted with some degree of mortification, had his mind been on driving. Instead he'd rehearsed over and over the scene with Jennifer in the hangar the night before.

His first instincts had been to berate himself for leaving her so hastily, but common sense came to his rescue very shortly and convinced him it was better this way. My God, she had been willing! The memory of her soft pliant body under his, holding him tightly, hungry for his kisses, almost unnerved him again.

He knew their desire for one another was a normal reaction. He'd read that many people, when faced with unexpected accidents or deaths in the family, have sudden insatiable sexual appetites. But to have taken advantage of the moment would have shattered what little self respect he had left.

Blaming Whitey's fall for his behavior was more cover-up, he knew. The truth was he had mixed feelings about a lot of things lately: his father, skydiving, Jennifer, to say nothing of Whitey's inexplicable decision to jump again after so many years. He felt as if his world were coming undone. He'd built his life the way he wanted it, with perfect control and order. He had his work, his friends, his lovers, and each knew its place and stayed there. Lately the glue was leaking out and his house of cards threatened to come tumbling down.

If he balked at making love to Jennifer the night before, perhaps it was because most of his unease stemmed from the day he met her. First he was uncommonly attracted to her. She was beautiful, but he'd had many beautiful women in his life, although not as many as the endless rumors had it. This one failed to react in the customary style, however. Not only that, she seemed so secure, so confident, so damned efficient! And worst of all, he found himself liking it. No, loving it. Loving her, perhaps. That was the last straw. He'd vowed never to fall in love.

It was because of Jennifer he'd thought about his father again. For some reason, ever since he'd told her to contact the old man for her opera promotion, he'd been thinking of him. Was he well? Did he still run Manning Enterprises with an iron hand? Who had he found to fill his, Colin's, shoes, to be groomed for the top spot?

Even skydiving failed to excite him anymore. Forced to look at the sport from Jennifer's perspective, he found it fun and challenging, but no longer the total reason for his existence. He'd felt a growing uneasiness inside, ever since Jennifer came into his life and made him question his lifestyle and his values.

And now Whitey! That was the final blow. That Whitey should suddenly decide to get back into jumping and then damn near kill himself, had pushed him over the edge, into behaving like a stupid ape. Thank God he had come to his senses in time. If not, he'd regret it the rest of his life.

Not that he didn't regret it anyway. She'd been eager enough. What harm would it have done? She'd never have to know he made love to her just because she was *there*, just to stop the pain in his head. She might forgive him, but he wouldn't forgive himself. She deserved better than that. When he made love to her, it would be because he wanted her and no one else. But the question remained: did he want her, or should he find his way back, somehow, to the life he had before?

He slammed his hastily-packed bag down on the worn sofa of the large living room, watching a small puff of dust swirl up. Well, at least he could be alone for a few days and think it through. His friend Hank never used this place in the summer. It was close to

Incline Village in Nevada and occupied only during ski season. He chuckled dryly. He'd better get in supplies. It might take the rest of the summer to solve *this* dilemma.

* * *

Colin could not be found. He was not at his apartment, nor the airport, nor even in the hospital visiting Whitey. Whenever Jennifer went there herself, she would ask if anyone had seen the tall, dark-haired skydiver, but she always received 'no' for an answer. If he came to visit his friend, he did it like a thief in the night and went undetected.

She hadn't even tried to contact Colin the first day after the accident. She was too embarrassed at first, and too much in love to trust herself to speak to him. She had no idea what she would say after the tormenting scene they had played out in the hangar that night.

But gradually her sensible nature

took precedence over her emotions, and she realized she had to find Colin and plan the last exhibition of the tour. She told Peter about the accident, and at first he seemed to be understanding, telling her to postpone the event until everyone had recovered from the shock.

Recovery, however, was slow. At the airport, activity all but halted. Whitey had been more than the airport manager, the trusted friend and driving force behind flying and skydiving at the field. He had been a fixture as well, someone who had seemed always to be there. Even men who had been flying or parachuting for many years couldn't remember when Whitey Franklin hadn't been around. Without him nothing ran smoothly or normally, and the uncertainty of his recovery shrouded every day with misery and lethargy. People stood around the hangar, talking in muffled tones, speculating on when, or if, Whitey would return.

Depressed, Jennifer stopped going

there, telephoning instead in her constant efforts to find Colin. Every day she telephoned and every day she heard the same report: Colin had not been seen, no one knew his whereabouts.

Then, a week later, George Manning called, telling her he had arranged for funding the opera promotion. The news, which should have overjoyed her, seemed merely ironic. Previously she would have been happy to have the opportunity to be free of the skydiving exhibition. Now it held no joy for her. She had not wanted it to end like this, with Whitey injured, Colin vanished, and her unexpected love for the man a burning, hard knot in the pit of her stomach.

Still, she knew she had to go on. If Colin couldn't be found, and it certainly seemed he had disappeared from the face of the earth, then the skydiving promotion would terminate, she would go on to the opera benefit, and somehow she would survive.

Peter, however, took the situation

almost as badly as Jennifer herself. 'How opportune,' he said to her one morning, standing in her office. 'The skydiving promotion is postponed because the head man has conveniently disappeared, and that leaves you free to do something you've preferred from the beginning.'

'That's not fair, Peter,' she said in a soft voice. Again she longed to tell him how terribly Colin's disappearance affected her. He cared about a mere promotion — she had lost a man she loved. And now, with him gone, she could never tell Peter the truth. 'You did promise me that I could have the opera promotion whenever the funds became available. Well, now they have. Colin's sudden withdrawal has nothing to do with that.'

'But how can anyone take it over when the star is gone?' he said.

'I'm sure he'll turn up eventually. Perhaps someone else will have better luck finding him than I did.'

'I don't see how anyone else could do

it, if you can't. After all, he's probably in love with you.'

She felt her face grow warm under his words, and the pain inside, which she had been trying hard to conquer, came back to torture her. 'That's not true,' she answered, although afraid she meant it. Even if Colin had been in love with her before, he had obviously changed his mind along the way. Perhaps the eagerness with which she responded to him in the hangar had been the very thing that drove him away.

* * *

Summer waned and Jennifer had to face reality — she would never be free of Colin. In spite of the fact that she never went near the airport anymore, and was finally working on her opera promotion, thoughts of him filled almost every waking moment. She'd been right all along: he only enjoyed the chase and didn't want anything serious to come of it. He didn't need her and there were plenty of other women who would be only too happy to take her place in his life. Probably he had found one already, and spent his evenings kissing her just as passionately as he'd once kissed her.

As if imagining those moments wasn't bad enough, she was reminded of him almost daily because of his father. George Manning was the liaison between herself and the source of funds for the opera promotion, and he was always in her office, breathing down her neck, acting as if she'd bungle everything connected with the performers, and especially the contractors working on the opera house, if he weren't there to give his unwanted advice.

She'd detected early on that he didn't really believe that. He was just hanging around because he enjoyed the excitement, the thrill of starting a new project and seeing it through to completion. The sort of thing he did every day of his life when he ran his many enterprises himself instead of letting a board of directors do it for him. He was a lot like Colin that way.

Unfortunately, he was a lot like Colin in looks, too, and she could hardly bear to see his fine, aristocratic features, his sparkling blue eyes, without visions of Colin looking just like that, tilting his head in that same way, grinning that same grin.

Why did she have to meet a skydiver? Why had she gone to meet his father and got him involved in her opera company? Of course, she had to admit that without his financial savvy, none of it might have materialized at all. She was also forced to admit that she liked the old man, and had learned a lot from him. But that was scant comfort to her when she felt plagued with longing and doubt.

To make matters worse, the elder Manning often asked questions about the skydiving promotion, and about the accident which had been headlined in the newspapers. Especially since Jennifer took time off, every two or three days, to go to the hospital to visit Whitey.

'You really liked him a great deal, didn't you?'

'I still do. Please don't speak of him in the past tense.'

'I guess my son was his friend, too.'

'More than his friend.' She stopped. Colin's feelings were not hers to reveal. But she could talk about Whitey. 'He was more than the airport manager. He was — is — a trusted friend to everyone, the person you can always rely on to do the right thing, say the right thing, keep the operation running smoothly.'

'But this skydiving nonsense,' Manning insisted, 'is stupid and dangerous, isn't it?'

'No, it's not. Lots of sports are dangerous, but the record of skydiving is a very good one. The parachute — ' she found herself explaining right out of the textbook, ' — is one of the safest pieces of equipment in the world.'

'Performed by a lot of crackpots and daredevils — '

'I've met a lot of skydivers in the past few weeks, and they're perfectly nice, ordinary people. Most of them have wives and children. I've met them. The married men are usually weekend jumpers and they spend their days at regular jobs. Some even head large companies.'

' — and totally unnecessary.'

'It's at least as worthy an occupation as mine. After all, skydiving is both a sport and a form of show business. As a promotion manager, I'm in show business, myself. I put on shows. And so are you now.' She softened her words with a smile.

'Opera is hardly in the same class with jumping from airplanes.' He arched his eyebrows and squared his shoulders, as if getting ready to do battle over their relative merits.

'Don't be a snob,' she teased, touching his hand, where he had outstretched it in a gesture of comparison. 'You like opera, some people like rock music. Skydiving may not be your cup of tea, but how about golf? I'll bet you played golf when you were a young man.'

'I play golf now,' he boasted. 'When I was a younger man, I rode a motorcycle.' The admission brought a flush to his otherwise fair skin.

'See.' She grinned at him and he grinned back.

Whatever he was going to say about his youthful escapades as a motorcyclist was interrupted by the appearance of Jennifer's boss, who came in holding some letters in his hand.

'Oh, excuse me,' Peter said, when he noticed her visitor.

'Don't mind me,' Manning said.

'Well, I do have work to do — ' Jennifer hoped Manning would take the hint and go off to badger someone else instead.

'Go ahead,' he said, sitting back in the armchair. 'I don't mind waiting.'

Peter took the man at his word and held up one of the letters. 'This is from the Awards Committee. You've won.'

'I don't understand. What have I won?'

'How could you forget? Your sports promotion at the Lido Lane Mall — the one you didn't want to do — ' he inserted, ' — has won first prize in the original events category.' He read from the single sheet of paper in his hand. ' 'The California Promotion Association annual award ceremony will be held at the Sheraton-Palace Hotel in San Francisco on September tenth,' and you're going to be presented with the statuette, the Stanley.'

Conflicting emotions raced through her at the news. In only her second year as a promotion director, she had won the coveted Stanley award.

'Well, say something,' Peter urged.

'I'm thrilled.' Lido Lane, the promotion where she'd met Colin, the one that might not have come off as well if he hadn't helped get the airplane onto the mall, was responsible for that.

'Let's see,' Peter mused, 'that's a Saturday night. We'll drive up to the city in the afternoon and I'll rent a suite for you at the Palace. You can get dressed there. I trust you have a fancy ball gown — every important person shows up for this event — and I'll dust off my tux — '

'I'm not going.'

'What?' Peter nearly dropped the letter. 'You have to go. Think of the prestige. Think of the benefit to Piedmont Productions.'

She knew he was right, that this was part of her job, too, yet she knew she'd be haunted by visions of Colin in that airplane, Colin walking on the mall with her, and everything that had followed as a result.

'Just a moment.' Manning stood up and faced Peter. 'If you're thinking of escorting Miss Gray to the festivities, think again. She'll be *my* guest. As you've pointed out, society will be out in force, and I know everyone who's anyone — '

Jennifer wanted to laugh. She already knew Manning enough to know he was pulling Peter's leg, doing his British royalty imitation, but she enjoyed it too much to interrupt. She shrugged and accepted the inevitable. She knew Manning would be in his element at such an event — she couldn't disappoint him. 'It will be my pleasure to go with you.'

Peter looked first at Jennifer and then Manning, shrugged, backed away toward the door, and then went through and closed it behind him.

'Well, my dear,' Manning said, beaming, 'it seems we have a 'date.' I don't know if you had any dates with my son while you managed his tour, but if not, the man is more of a fool than I thought.' On that note, he did his Prince Charming bow and left.

Jennifer, meanwhile, had been attracted to the second envelope, which lay unopened on her desk. It had no return address at all, and the handwriting, bold and upright, commanded her attention. Not bothering to reach for her letter opener, she thrust a fingernail into the edge of the flap and ripped it aside. A check fell out, but she let it drop while she read the few scrawled words on the accompanying page.

'Dear Miss Gray,' it read. 'I regret that I am unable to continue with my part of the skydiving exhibitions. Please accept the enclosed check, which is the return of the fee paid to me so far, and my apologies. I am giving up skydiving and leaving the area. I trust you will be able to find someone to take my place. Colin Thomas.'

She dropped heavily into the chair, letting the paper fall to the floor. Her face felt tight and tears clouded her eyes. What difference did winning the Stanley Award make now? It wouldn't bring Colin back. She'd lost him forever.

20

Jennifer's next few weeks became even busier, impossible though that seemed, than the preceding ones had been. Although the paperwork and forms had lessened, the opera benefit entailed far more in the way of telephone calls and personal visits with the people involved.

Each evening she collapsed into bed, weary to her very bones, yet realizing that the tired feelings stemmed as much from her depressed mood as the work. She found herself desperate for sleep as soon as she had finished dinner, yawning and scarcely able to keep her eyes open. Then she retired and slept soundly until the clock radio woke her at seven the next morning. When she thought of it, she speculated that her body recognized the painful thoughts she harbored whenever strict attention to business was over, and protected her by bringing the warm unconsciousness of sleep.

Occasionally she was asked out on a date, but she never accepted those invitations. Knowing she loved Colin made everyone else seem bland and uninteresting by comparison. Her head told her that, since she couldn't have Colin, she might as well get over him as quickly as possible, but still she balked at the idea.

* * *

The awards ceremony took place the second week of September, and Jennifer and George Manning drove to San Francisco together early in the day. Although she had been to the city several times before, Jennifer allowed Manning to play tour guide and they drove the winding turns of Lombard Street in his limousine, visited the quaint shops in Ghiradelli Square and even went up to Telegraph Hill and looked out at the sailboats on the bay.

She approved of the choice of San Francisco in September, a beautiful month in the city. The summer could sometimes be cold, with fog coming in from the ocean to blanket the streets, but autumn held warm, sunny days and balmy nights, right up to the beginning of the rainy season.

At five o'clock they arrived at the Sheraton-Palace and went directly to the suite provided by the awards committee. Jennifer closeted herself in her bedroom and changed into the other clothes she had brought. Removing the blazer and slacks she wore for their day on the town, she dressed in a long gown of blue silk, with hand-painted flowers and butterflies extending from just above her waist on the left side, down the entire straight length of the skirt and around the border of the hem. The dress had spaghetti-thin straps and a shawl of the same fabric, and her silk shoes had been dyed to match the blue of the dress. Her blonde hair, brushed to a shiny mane, framed her face, and a small strand of real pearls that had been in her family for years, constituted her only jewelry.

The intake of his breath, when Manning saw her, told her she'd made a stunning effect on him, and she shoved to the back of her mind the sudden longing to have Colin be the man standing in front of her.

Together with other promotion managers, many of whom Jennifer had met before, they entered the Garden Court ballroom, its vaulted ceiling topped with leaded glass windows, its many chandeliers sparkling, and found seats at the round white cloth-covered tables. Everyone had dressed especially for the gala occasion, the ladies in formal gowns, the men in tuxedos. Like so many of the events they promoted, this too benefitted charity, and, besides the promotion firms and their employees, a large number of prominent society people from the bay area attended.

Manning pointed out a famous columnist from the San Francisco

Chronicle to Jennifer, and she recognized a well-known society woman from Hillsborough, a town on the peninsula, at a nearby table, amply adorned with diamonds.

The lavish dinner, everything Jennifer could have desired, went largely untouched, and she felt more nervous and upset than the occasion warranted. Although Whitey continued to make progress in the hospital and she had been assured on her latest visit that he would be released soon, she still could not shake the depression which clung to her every waking moment.

Nothing in the program which followed the dinner did anything to alleviate her mood. She listened to speeches by members of the governing board of the California Promotion Managers and the various charities which benefitted from the awards contest every year, followed by film clips of the promotions that had been nominated for awards. When scenes of her own promotion came on the screen,

Jennifer was startled to see how very good it looked on film. But, except for the leaden weight in her stomach, she felt nothing. Finally the lights went up again, and several pretty young girls carried the silver statuettes, the Stanleys, to a table near the microphone.

The lights seemed unbearably bright, and she felt as if every eye scrutinized her as she allowed Peter to escort her to the front of the room. There the president of the association made a brief, complimentary speech and then put the silver figure into Jennifer's trembling hands. Its smooth surface cold under her fingers, its weight surprising her, she glanced at it for some moments before smiling to the audience and approaching the microphone. She made a brief acceptance speech, words tumbling out without conscious thought. She made her way back to the table, and sank into her chair.

'Congratulations,' Manning said, squeezing her hand. 'I gather this is the Promotion

Association equivalent of the Oscars and Tonys.'

'Probably the highest I'll ever get,' she joked, taking a sip of water to quench her sudden thirst. Her throat felt as dry as the Mojave Desert.

'By the way, there's something I've been meaning to tell you,' Manning said.

'What is it?' she asked. But, before he could answer, the dance orchestra began to play, the Association chairman came up and whisked her to the dance floor. The music was a waltz and he whirled her around until she almost felt dizzy. Then, suddenly, she felt pulled away and found herself in Colin's arms.

She could only stare in disbelief. How did he come to be there?

'You are absolutely gorgeous,' he said, 'although I've always thought so, even in that second-hand yellow jump-suit you wore to ground school.'

She had to smile at that, but words still eluded her.

'Congratulations on your award,' he said.

Struck speechless by his appearance, she could only smile foolishly, feeling that her unspoken prayers had been answered. It had been so long, and he seemed different. He wore a black dinner jacket, but it looked as correct on him as his usual jumpsuit always did. Every dark hair of his head lay perfectly in place.

Suddenly, Peter cut in, apparently not recognizing Colin, and whirled her off like a speeding taxi.

'Let go,' she muttered. Unable to release herself from Peter's tight hold, she looked around for Colin, but he had disappeared as mysteriously as he had appeared. 'Let me go,' she said again, pushing as hard as she could.

Reluctantly, Peter released her and her gaze made a complete circle of the room. No Colin. Had she only dreamed his presence? She staggered back to the table, where Manning sat. 'Where — ?'

He ignored her question, took her hand and forced her into a chair. 'As I started to say, there's something I have to tell you.' He paused. 'It's about Colin.'

'What about him? Where is he? I thought you disowned him, didn't want to talk about him or see him anymore.'

'I've changed my mind.'

Jennifer stared into Manning's face. 'Do you mean that?'

'I've done a lot of thinking lately about what you told me. And I've come to like you very much and respect your judgment. If *you* could fall in love with him, he must have turned out pretty well.'

She felt her face flush. 'I'm glad you've changed your mind about what he does, but what makes you think I'm in love with him?'

'It's been in your voice and your eyes every time you talk about him. Sometimes, when you think I'm not looking, your face takes on a dreamy quality and I know you're thinking about him.'

She might as well admit it. 'Even if you're right, that doesn't mean Colin and I should — could — '

'See! Nobody wants a skydiver, especially not a crazy one like him.'

'He's not crazy,' she defended, just as vehement as he. 'He's the most caring, intelligent, sensitive man I've ever met. He's not just good as his sport. He runs the best skydiving school in the country. With the best safety record, too. And skydiving isn't foolish and dangerous. It requires concentration, coordination, attention to details, and the people who practice it are wonderful, witty, charming people you'd be proud to call your friends.'

She stopped again, another truth dawning on her. She had just admitted that she admired everything about him. Although she knew she loved him, she'd given little thought to their future together. Now she realized she no longer considered skydiving the ultimate stupidity. No longer cringed at the thought of spending her life with someone who taught people how to parachute. So what if skydiving occupied his entire life? She wouldn't try to change him. She'd accepted him for himself at last, talked away all her own prejudices. Nothing more remained to hold her back.

But where was Colin?

* * *

George Manning appeared at Jennifer's office early on Monday morning. He sat down in the chair opposite her desk and, wasting no time on civilities, announced. 'I want to reconcile with my son.'

'I think reconciliation is a very good thing. I suspected as much when you spoke about him at the banquet.'

'The problem is,' he went on, 'I can't find him. I have his address. I always thought I could reach him quickly if I really needed to. He didn't know that, of course,' he added. 'But now he has suddenly disappeared and the private detectives I hired haven't a clue to his whereabouts. I have no doubt they'll find him eventually, but I don't want to wait. You've been working with him. Do you know where he is?'

'I don't think I can help you,' Jennifer said. She told him how Colin had shown up at the banquet and then disappeared again. 'Except for that, I haven't seen Colin in weeks. No one has.'

'But you will try, won't you?' He leaned forward, his hands reaching out to clasp hers. 'You know more of these skydivers and can get information that perhaps the detectives can't. I will pay you, of course, the same rate I pay the detectives.'

'I wouldn't dream of accepting payment,' Jennifer said. 'I've been looking for him too . . . ' She paused. 'You see, you were right the other night. I'm in love with your son. I thought he cared for me too, but evidently not.' She paused, watching the man's reaction.

His face underwent a series of small

changes, ending with a smile. 'Thank you for telling me. I'm sure it wasn't easy. But please learn from my mistakes. Don't give up on him, as I once did. If you find him, you'll earn the undying gratitude of an old man, and a foolish father.'

He sat back in the chair again. 'I should never have allowed this rift to occur in the first place.'

'I'm sure you did your best,' Jennifer said, trying to soothe him.

'No, not really. Oh, at first, I was all in the right and he in the wrong — at least that's what I thought — but that's small consolation to me now. I'm the one who should have broken the long silence. I was older and supposedly wiser, but I was too stubborn . . . '

'People are not always as wise as they should be. We're only human.' She remembered too clearly the episode in the hangar. 'I don't know what good it will do, but there's one other lead I can try, if you'll help me.'

'What is it?'

'Your niece Billie might know where to find Colin.' Jennifer related the bare facts of her meetings with the girl at the lake exhibition. 'I'll call her now, if I may.'

Jennifer dialed the number Manning gave her, but Billie had no idea that Colin hadn't kept to his usual routine.

'He called last week and asked if I wanted to go to a fancy dinner party for charity but I said no. I haven't heard from him since.'

'Thanks anyway, Billie. If you do hear from him again, please tell him to call his father immediately. It's important.'

When she gave Manning the news, the man sighed heavily and rose to his feet. 'Thank you again. You must call me the moment you hear anything.'

At the door, he turned and spoke again. 'You are such a beautiful woman. I don't wonder my son fell in love with you. You look exactly as I would wish a daughter-in-law to look, golden and full of light and warmth. I could have such lovely grandchildren . . . '

After he left, Jennifer wracked her brain, wondering where to look for Colin. She had to find him now for his father's sake as well as her own. But how? She had exhausted all the possibilities long ago.

As if from habit, her compact car turned off when she came to the road leading to the airport, and she parked in the lot adjacent to the Skyway Aviation building and went inside. The deserted office even smelled unused and she wandered around, reading all the messages on the bulletin board, searching through the things on the desk, as if somehow a clue to Colin's whereabouts would leap into focus before her eyes.

Even if such a clue existed, it hardly seemed possible in that place. It was, after all, Whitey's office and Whitey's desk. On almost all of her many visits to him in the hospital, she had asked Whitey if he had any thoughts on the subject, but with no success. He mentioned some places Colin might go, but none of the leads had turned up the man himself. Whitey's desk contained merely his own mail, most of which had been opened by someone else in his absence so as not to overlook anything of importance. Skewered to the spindle in the corner was a single sheet of paper, a list in his own handwriting, of jumps he planned to make after his decision to return to skydiving. As she scanned the list, Jennifer sighed heavily. It had turned out to be a short-lived second career.

At last she left the airport, lunched, and then returned to her own office. Time didn't stand still while she attempted to solve the riddle of Colin's disappearance. The stack of mail on her desk, literally a foot high, contained much that headed straight for the wastebasket. The very nature of her job ensured that she would be on almost every mailing list for books, magazines, gift catalogues, and specialty advertising, and now the opera promotion generated its own paperwork.

Amidst all of that, reminders of the skydiving promotion took up more space. It seemed she had got herself on every parachute club mailing list in just the few short weeks she had been involved in the sport. At first she wanted to hurl the material into the round file as well, and then thought better of it. If someone else ever decided to do a skydiving tour, he might need some of the flyers, invitations and information. She sorted through it and made a neat pile on one corner of her desk. She would ask her secretary to file it before she left the building.

Hastily, she sorted the remaining sheets of paper, giving a quick reading to the ones pertaining to the opera promotion, to be sure she hadn't neglected anything important, until at last she finished and could go home.

She rose wearily from the chair and stretched, arching her arms high above her head to relieve the tension in her back. Then she swung her head up and down slowly to stretch her neck muscles. The pile of papers on skydiving came into focus when she tilted her head downward. 'Pleasant Hill,' she read in large flowery script, and underneath it, 'Tracy Air Field.'

It triggered her memory. Pleasant Hill had been the first thing written on the list she had seen on Whitey's desk only hours ago. Then, halfway down the list of events, as if leaping from the page at her, she read 'Whitey Franklin.' Her heart lurched at the sight of the familiar name. He must have signed up for it before the accident. She picked up the sheet of paper and examined it more closely. The event would be held on Saturday, the very next day! But surely they knew about the accident. Probably they hadn't had time to take his name off the flyers before they mailed them out.

She dropped the sheet of paper on the desk again and started to leave the room. But what if they didn't know?

She turned and picked up the flyer

again. She saw no address or telephone number, merely the name of the parachute club sponsoring the event. It would have to do. She picked up the telephone and after seven calls and twenty minutes, she spoke to the man in charge of Saturday's event.

'You don't know me,' Jennifer began, 'but I have a copy of your flyer about the meet at Tracy Air Field this Saturday, and I wanted to ask a question.'

'Sure,' the pleasant male voice on the other end replied. 'What can I do for you?'

'I'd like to discuss one of the jumpers, Whitey Franklin.'

Jennifer held the line while the man apparently looked up something. 'Oh, yes,' he resumed, 'from Stafford, a new skydiver, I understand.'

'Not really, he used to jump years ago. Anyway, the point is, he won't be jumping tomorrow. I thought you ought to know in case he hadn't informed you himself.'

'No, he hadn't. In fact, I just talked to him the other day and he assured me he would be here.'

Jennifer's mouth dropped open in surprise and she couldn't find her voice for some seconds. 'He called and said he would be there?'

'No, he didn't call, he came here in person.'

'But that's impossible!' Jennifer sputtered into the phone. 'The man is in the hospital with multiple injuries . . . '

'Are you sure we're talking about the same man, lady?'

'Yes, Whitey Franklin, a medium-sized man of about sixty, thick white hair. That's where he gets his name.'

'Well, the Whitey Franklin I saw the other day is thirtyish, tall, and had dark curly hair.'

Jennifer's heart almost stopped beating. It was Colin. It had to be! Why had he pretended to be Whitey? What reason could he have? 'Tell me,' she said quickly, 'where can I reach this man? Do you have a telephone number or an address?'

'There's an address here somewhere,' he said, accompanied by sounds of papers rustling. 'Here it is, Skyway Aviation.'

'I have that,' Jennifer said. 'What about a telephone number?' She recognized the number he recited to her as that of Whitey's office at the field.

'Sorry, Miss, but you can see him jump on Saturday.'

'Yes, I guess I'll have to,' she answered. 'Thank you very much.'

Fairly flying, she raced from the office and down the hallway to the exit. She would drive to Pleasant Hill at once and then to Tracy Air Field.

But what if it wasn't Colin, after all? It had to be though — it just had to be. Colin would do something like that, take Whitey's place. Her pounding heart told her so.

21

Jennifer awakened with a start, the hot sun warm on her face, and knew it was very late. Tossing the covers aside, she reached for her watch, and discovered what she had suspected — it was almost nine o'clock.

All during her hurried shower, and while pulling on the same slacks and blouse she had worn the day before, she berated herself for trusting the motel office to wake her in time. When she had gone to bed in the Easy-Rest Motel the night before, she had thought nothing could keep her asleep past dawn, so she could rush to the air field before the activities started, find Colin and give him the message from his father. But sleep had eluded her.

After the swift packing, then driving all the way to Pleasant Hill, she had registered at the motel, given them the instructions to wake her at 6:30 in the morning and then tried to sleep. But she had tossed and turned for hours. Her active brain replayed the conversation she had had with the man on the telephone, replayed her conversation with Mr. Manning about wanting to see his son, and, worst of all, had played, over and over, variations on the theme of what she would say to Colin when she finally saw him.

Then, as if to torment her more completely, she had relived the moments when she had been with Colin. She had flopped onto her stomach, pulling the pillow over her head, as if this would shut out the scenes she no longer wished visualized in her head, but then she turned again, flung the blankets from her body and hoped for sleep to spirit her away into unconsciousness. When it had finally come, it had taken a drug-like form, with the result that she had slept too soundly, her usual rising hour had come and gone.

A map of the area on the seat beside

her, purchased during a hasty stop at a service station, Jennifer drove as fast as she dared, eyes constantly scanning the sides of the highway, watching for signs to the air field. At last it came into sight, and the many cars already parked in the gravel-covered lot told her she was dreadfully late.

She told herself she could just as easily find Colin after the events, that if he intended to jump in Whitey's place, he wouldn't go anywhere until he had done that and she could talk to him then. Yet, what if he left the area somehow without her knowledge? She paid her entrance fee and walked purposefully toward the hangar, trying to look as if she knew her way around so that no one would stop her.

Inside, everyone looked alike, as usual, all dressed in jumpsuits, helmets and goggles, fastening on two parachutes. She looked for the tallest man, but some hunched over equipment, others sat tying on their boots or athletic shoes, and she had to circle the room before she spotted Colin, her heart leaping into her throat.

He saw her at the same moment and his eyes first widened in surprise, then narrowed, as if he had no wish to see her there. She approached him timidly, stared into his familiar face, all the rehearsed speeches from the night before forgotten. She longed to stretch on her tiptoes and plant a kiss on that mouth, remembering how it had claimed hers on so many occasions, the sweet hard pressure of it.

She wrenched her thoughts back to the present. 'Colin, please listen. I have to talk to you.'

'I haven't time,' he answered tersely. 'How did you find me, anyway?'

'I saw Whitey's name on a flyer for this exhibition and when I called they said he would jump. I knew — that is, I suspected — you came to take his place.'

Colin glanced away from her, buckling his harness more tightly. 'That was very clever of you, but I don't have time to talk right now.'

Jennifer had hoped he'd be overjoyed to see her, but perhaps that was unrealistic. She returned to her mission. 'I had to find you, not just for myself, but . . . '

'I don't expect you to understand,' he interrupted, his tone softening, 'but I had to do this.'

'But I do understand. I know how much you care for Whitey.'

He frowned again. 'That had nothing to do with it. I wanted to jump and I couldn't do it under my own name. Besides,' he added, 'after all these years I can't just quit skydiving overnight. You don't know what it's like. Once you've been up there . . . '

'It's true I haven't jumped,' Jennifer said, 'and I guess I don't understand the attraction it has for you, but I'm also sure that's not your entire reason. You'd rather die than let anyone think you have an altruistic thought, but I remember all you told me that night after Whitey's accident. You tried to protect Whitey's name, to make a jump that would go down in the books as his, didn't you?'

He didn't answer, but turned and left the hangar.

Jennifer realized that all the other jumpers had already gone, and she hurried after him, clutching the sleeve of his white jumpsuit. 'Colin, wait, I haven't told you why I came. It's terribly important.'

She ran to keep up with his long strides across the field. 'It's your father.'

He stopped in his tracks, forcing her to do the same, and they looked at one another. 'What about my father?'

'He needs you. He asked me to find you. He wants to make peace with you, ask you to forgive him.'

Colin's head turned and he watched the others, now far from him, boarding helicopters and planes that would take them aloft. 'I have to go. I'll be down in ten minutes.'

But Jennifer felt as if she would never see him again if she let him leave her then. 'I'm going with you.'

Colin continued walking. 'No, you're not. You're afraid of heights. This is not a Greyhound bus you know.'

'I know. I also know I came close to losing you. If I have to fly in an airplane to prove I love you, I'm ready.'

After a long moment, he said, 'Wait right here.' He ran back to the hangar and returned with an extra parachute over his arm. Then he took her hand and led her to the plane. 'The pilot's ready to start. Time to go.'

Her heart seemed to be smashing against her ribs like a metronome gone berserk, but she kept smiling. 'I guess so.'

He boosted her up into the open side door and she found herself in a large empty space behind the single pilot. Then Colin thrust the spare parachute at her. Perspiration forming beads on her forehead, hands fumbling nervously, she opened the harness and stepped into it. Colin helped her, buckling it tightly into position.

'Greyhound buses might not need this, or even a cruise ship, but I'm taking no chances with you.' Next he sat her down onto the bench inside the plane, fastened her seat belt, then sat next to her and fastened his own.

The engine sprang into life and they began to taxi forward. So far, so good. She didn't feel the least bit giddy. But then, she'd done this much before.

The runway appeared and the pilot turned onto it. He pulled the mike to his mouth and said something to the control tower, continued to taxi into position. Then he pushed the throttle all the way forward and the plane tore down the runway. Jennifer's heart seemed about to leap out of her chest. But suddenly the sense of motion disappeared. They were in the air.

Looking out the front window, she saw only blue sky and puffy white clouds in the distance, but no sensation of moving. It was if she were sitting in a giant rocking chair in the sky. She looked out the open door on the side and saw the land drop away beneath them. Rectangular patches of color — greens, browns, golds — replaced the runway that had been below a moment before, and they flew over the nearby farms and fields. It was just like the balloon flight, only with more control. And noise.

Colin reached out and took her hand. 'I love you.'

Her heart pounding, she only grinned. 'You're just saying that because I'm such a daredevil.'

'I only have a few minutes,' he said. 'Tell me exactly what my father said. Is something the matter? Is he sick?'

'Your father is all right,' she said, putting her hand over his. 'But he wants to see you. He wants to tell you he forgives you, and to ask you to forgive him for the way he acted. He said he wished he had done it years ago. He admitted he'd been a stubborn old man.'

'Stubborn!' Colin repeated, flinging the word out and raising his eyes upward for a moment. 'I'm the stubborn one! And a fool!'

'No, you mustn't blame yourself. You did try to see him. He knows that.' She wished she could say more, but having to shout her words over the din of the engine made it difficult.

'It's really funny,' Colin said. 'Do you know that I planned to see him tomorrow anyway?'

'You did?'

'He hasn't been out of my thoughts for two minutes ever since I left you that night. Finally I decided I had to go back and see him. And now I find he wants to see me too.'

He got to his feet, pulling on gloves, but his face showed an inner torture and agony. 'I have to go now.' Then, his rough hands pulled her from her perch and crushed her against the reserve parachute strapped to his chest.

'I have no right to do this,' he shouted over the noise of the aircraft, 'but I may never see you again. I love you but I don't deserve you.' His lips descended on hers and for a moment she lost herself in the thrill. Then he pulled away, and stared questioningly at her face. 'Why are you crying? What's wrong?'

'I'm not crying,' Jennifer lied, and she tried to smile but the corners of her mouth refused to behave.

'You're crying,' he insisted. 'Please don't. You're only making it harder for me. I can reconcile with my father, but what am I to do about you? I've loved you ever since the first time I saw you in a jumpsuit. I want to marry you, Jennifer. I haven't the right to say that, because you ought to marry some Brooks Brothers type with a normal job, but I think I knew you would become the only woman in my life since the day we met. You were so sure of yourself, so sparkling and efficient and beautiful.' He kissed her again, holding her so tightly she thought her breathing would stop.

He kissed her again, then released his lips from hers and his arms from their firm grip on her. 'Good-bye, my love,' he said,

But Jennifer's thumping heart only heard what he had said before, that he loved her. She threw her arms around his neck and screamed over the noise of the engine. 'I don't want anyone else. I love you. I've loved you since the day at the lake when I thought you were drowning.'

'You love me? At the least I've been the world's biggest fool, but I'll try not to be anymore. I'm working on becoming human again, Jennifer, I really am. I'll give up skydiving, go back to my father's business, make you proud of me.'

'I'm proud of you now. I want you just the way you are.'

The pilot intruded. 'Will you please jump?' he yelled.

'I can't leave you,' she said. 'Let me jump with you.'

As if he could not tear his gaze from her face, Colin stared adoringly at her. 'What, you're not afraid to jump?'

'I took all the ground school training. I'm ready. Besides, I can't be without you. I'm not afraid. If you love me, I can do anything!'

The pilot yelled again. Apparently making up his mind in an instant, Colin quickly removed his helmet and goggles, putting them on Jennifer's head. 'Here, you need these more than I do.'

After he strapped the helmet beneath her chin, he leaned forward and kissed her again.

'Do you remember everything?'

'Yes,' she breathed, her ecstasy over knowing they loved one another completely obliterating even a hint of fear for doing something she had once vowed she would never attempt.

'I'm going to be with you almost every second. We're going together. I'll hold your hand, and I'll stay with you until you open your 'chute. I'll free fall farther and then open mine lower down so that I'll land first. Then I can be on the ground first and catch you.'

'I know how to fall,' Jennifer said, her voice sounding strange through the helmet. 'You taught me.'

He laughed, then took a firm grip on her hand and led her to the open doorway. He looked down and got his bearings on the field below. Placing his free hand on the doorway, he leaned out, then tugged gently on Jennifer's arm, helping her toward the door.

Colin's gaze caught hers again and he nodded his head. 'Now,' he shouted.

They leaped into space together, and, as if she had been doing it all her life, Jennifer arched her body and stretched out her arms and legs in the stable position. She thought her heart would burst through her chest with exhilaration. She was flying!

The wind whipped at her clothes, filling her with an icy chill. But the incredible beauty of the azure sky, with no clouds anywhere in sight, the ground beneath checkered into patches of green, brown and yellow, calmed her.

She heard no sound — felt no

sensation of falling — only the faint hiss of air past her helmet, and the tug of wind against her slacks and sleeves, but she felt free as a bird, soaring through the silken sky like a butterfly. She wanted to sing, but her breath seemed to be suspended and she couldn't make a sound. It was the supreme flying experience, like conquering the world. It trivialized everything else in her entire life.

No wonder skydivers loved the sport! No wonder they delayed opening their parachutes as long as possible, never wanting time to end their feelings of being exempted from the laws of gravity, floating through air like creatures from another planet.

Colin's grip on her hand tightened and she looked at him and found his eyes searching hers, his lips smiling. She grinned at him in return, wishing she could say all the things that raced through her mind, yet knowing that he understood. He of all people understood.

All too soon he signalled for her to

pull her ripcord. Was the ground really that close? It didn't seem to be coming up rapidly at all. She didn't want the spectacular moment to end. She grasped the metal handle, and when he nodded to her, she pulled it, but nothing happened and she looked up at Colin in surprise. The ring came away in her hands, little wires attached to it, but she continued to float. Then suddenly, she was snatched upward and out of Colin's handclasp, and felt as if her arms were being torn out of their sockets.

She looked at the canopy above: all the colors of the rainbow. Perfect! None of the things that could go wrong had happened. She almost felt cheated of the opportunity to practice what she had learned about emergencies. But she remembered Colin had told her that was only a 'once-in-a-lifetime' possibility.

Holding tightly on the lines, she looked down. Colin continued to free fall, and then, before her eyes, his parachute began to deploy and he disappeared beneath its huge striped canopy. What an odd sensation, seeing a parachute below you instead of above.

The ground came up at her at increasingly faster speeds. The patches gave way to one large brown area — the drop zone — and then she had to remember how to land, how to fall and roll so as not to injure herself. Calf, thigh, buttocks, shoulder, she repeated, and remembered the many times she'd practiced it.

But she needn't have worried about doing it properly that day. Colin stood beneath her and, with a thud, she crashed into him and the two of them went tumbling over and over in the dirt, tangled in the parachutes, laughing and kissing all at once.

* * *

Near the hangar, Colin's father and Jennifer's mother stood on the gras waiting to greet the newly weds a their second free fall together.

'That was wonderful,' Mr. Manning said.

'Are you ready to try it too?' Colin asked, hugging his father.

The older man laughed heartily. 'No, but I'm resigned to the fact that I'll probably have a lot of skydiving grandchildren.' He gave Mrs. Gray a knowing wink. They'd become good friends in the week since the wedding.

'That's if you let me have time off from running your business to give them lessons,' Colin said.

'I have a feeling you'll make time. Anyway,' he added, 'you don't have to work for me if you don't want to. That was your own idea, remember? Won't you miss aviation?'

'The teaching, flying, jumping? Yes. The paperwork and details, no. Now that he's back, I'm going to sell the business to Whitey. Didn't he look great at the ceremony?'

'He once told me it's been his life-long dream to own his own aviation service,' Jennifer added.

'As for me,' Colin continued, 'I'm ready to become a Manning again. It will be a new challenge. Skydiving will just be my hobby from now on.'

'I worried so about you. What did you do all those weeks when no one could find you?' She searched his face with adoring eyes and held his strong hand in a tight grip.

'I went to a little cabin in the mountains. I think I knew a long time ago that I would have to come to grips with my life sooner or later, but I still kept fighting it. First I had to forgive myself for thinking my father had taken my mother away from me.'

'But he didn't.' She squeezed his hand for emphasis.

'I know that now. In fact, I'd already begun to realize my attitude toward my father was childish and unrealistic. Then when Whitey fell, I knew I had to confront my feelings. It seemed as if I'd already lost my father, and then I came close to losing Whitey too. It was too much. Especially on top of falling in love with you.'

She rested her head on his shoulder. 'I'm so glad you and your father are together again. And I'm happy for us.'

'No more than I am. After a couple of weeks of soul-searching I felt like a new person. I made my peace over my mother and Whitey, and now I have you.'

'Well, I hope you won't mind if I make a few jumps,' Jennifer said. 'I hate to eat humble pie, but I must retract everything I ever said about it being a stupid sport. I know I'll never look up at the sky again without remembering how it feels to fly through it.'

Colin took her into his arms. 'There's no thrill quite like it.'

She held him tightly, closed her eyes for his kiss. Let him think that if he wanted to. Personally, loving him was just as great a thrill. Yes, she decided, a free fall was a lot like being in love.

Other titles in the
Linford Romance Library:

TOMORROW'S DREAMS

Chrissie Loveday

Nellie is a talented paintress in the pottery industry of the 1920s. Disaster strikes the family, and she becomes the main breadwinner for her parents and three siblings. But the fates conspire against her and she is forced to seek employment where she can find it. She loses her heart to the wrong man and he, recognising her special talents, offers her a future. But how could she ever move into his world?

TO LOVE AGAIN

Fenella Miller

Since she was widowed, it has been difficult for Emma Reed and her young children, Jack and Mary. But then, Rupert Bucknall offers her a job as his housekeeper. However things do not go well. Rupert has a fearsome temper and doesn't want her or the children to remain. Since his accident Rupert has lived as a recluse, believing his scars make him hideous. But Emma, with nowhere to go, must persuade Mr Bucknall that she is indispensable.

HERE COMES THE BRIDE

Kat Parkhurst

Isobel's sister is getting married and wants her to be a bridesmaid. How hard can it be? Very hard, it seems, as bride-to-be, Kelly, lurches from one disaster to the next. Isobel tries to help, but her own relationship is threatened, her beloved granddad ends up in hospital, and then she has a car accident. She begins to wonder if the wedding will ever take place — and if she would be in any condition to be a bridesmaid . . .

A FAMILY AFFAIR

Catriona McCuaig

The Great War brings sadness for Nurse Emma Meadows and her parents: her brother has an accident while learning to fly a biplane, and after a neighbour spurns her, their young sister runs away from home. Emma, herself, loves Dr James Townsend and when he is reported dead on active service in France she goes there to learn the truth of his death — little knowing what she will find when she gets there.

FOOL'S PARADISE

Teresa Ashby

Karen Scott and her twin brother, Travis, travel to the Virgin Islands to study a coral reef and make a documentary film. However, Karen's fiancé, Jeremy, is furious and breaks off their engagement. Meanwhile, Karen falls for another diver, Ross Allen, but when he finds out about her fiancé back home, he suggests that she still has feelings for Jeremy . . . When the filming is over, will Karen return home with her brother, or will she stay with Ross?